A SAD MOMENT

"Does this *nothing* have a name?" she asked.

He swallowed and nodded. "Yes."

She was having trouble breathing. "Do I know her name?"

"Yes."

She choked. "Oh God."

Bill rolled over and took hold of her shoulders. There was pain on his face, but he was no mirror for her because her pain was beyond comprehension. When he spoke, his words sounded so stupid he should have kept his mouth shut.

"I didn't want to hurt you," he said.

"You can't want her instead of me," she whispered.

"Teresa, I didn't *want* any of this."

"Does she know?"

He raised his voice. "Of course she knows! She feels the same way I do. I'm telling you, we didn't want this to happen."

Teresa felt herself going into shock. Her mind couldn't keep up with how fast her heart was sinking. "What happened?" she cried. "What have you two been doing together?"

"Nothing. I swear to you, nothing's happened yet."

She felt so exposed, so used. " 'Yet'?" she croaked. "Is something going to happen?"

Books by Christopher Pike

BURY ME DEEP
CHAIN LETTER 2: THE ANCIENT EVIL
DIE SOFTLY
FALL INTO DARKNESS
FINAL FRIENDS #1: THE PARTY
FINAL FRIENDS #2: THE DANCE
FINAL FRIENDS #3: THE GRADUATION
GIMME A KISS
LAST ACT
MASTER OF MURDER
MONSTER
REMEMBER ME
ROAD TO NOWHERE
SCAVENGER HUNT
SEE YOU LATER
SPELLBOUND
WHISPER OF DEATH
WITCH

Available from ARCHWAY Paperbacks

Christopher Pike

Road to Nowhere

AN ARCHWAY PAPERBACK
Published by POCKET BOOKS

New York   London   Toronto   Sydney   Tokyo   Singapore

The song "Until Then" is used with permission of Paul Dorado, copyright 1992.

AN ARCHWAY PAPERBACK *Original*

An Archway Paperback published by
POCKET BOOKS, a division of Simon & Schuster Inc.
1230 Avenue of the Americas, New York, NY 10020

ISBN: 0-671-74508-5

First Archway Paperback printing March 1993

10 9 8 7 6 5 4 3 2 1

AN ARCHWAY PAPERBACK and colophon are registered trademarks of Simon & Schuster Inc.

Cover art by Brian Kotzky

Printed in the U.S.A.

IL 14+

For My Mother

Road to Nowhere

CHAPTER 1

LIGHTNING FLASHED IN TERESA CHAFEY'S EYES AS SHE slammed the apartment door shut. The night air was cold. Thick clouds and thunder rolled in from the west. Rain began to fall. Teresa paused for a moment. Maybe she should go back inside, she thought, get her raincoat, her umbrella. Or maybe she should go back inside and stay inside. It was kind of late to run away from home.

But she didn't want to go back into the apartment. She had her reasons.

Teresa hurried toward the carport. The rain splashed her light brown hair, plastering the fine strands to her cheeks. But her face had been wet long before the rain touched it. She had been crying, and still was.

So many reasons to cry.

Her parents were away for the weekend. She stood in their empty parking place as she fumbled in her pockets for her car keys. Her mom and dad were in San Diego visiting her older brother, his wife, and

1

their new baby—her niece, Kathy. They had wanted Teresa to go with them, but she had said she was too busy. They never called when they were away. She'd be long gone before they came home.

Her car was a red Mazda 626—four years old, in excellent shape. She opened the door and tossed an overnight bag in the backseat. She had packed little: stuff from her bathroom; an extra sweater; a change of underwear; her checkbook. She didn't have much cash, maybe ninety bucks. She'd get a job—it would do until then. She climbed into the car and started the engine and pulled out of the carport. She wouldn't be coming back, not for anything.

Teresa headed for the exit at the opposite end of the apartment complex. Turning onto the road, she aimed for the freeway, six miles away. She had no clear idea where she wanted to end up, except that her general direction was north. Maybe up the coast—it would be nice to have the ocean as a companion along the way. She lived in Los Angeles and thought she might not stop driving until she got to Canada. No one would find her there. Bill would think she'd died. She smiled at the thought. The bastard—let him sweat.

Bill was one of the reasons she was running away.

But not her only one, nor her biggest.

Teresa rolled down the window as she drove. She should have been cold with the rain rushing in, but she felt warm. She was actually sweating, as if she had a fever. The cold rain and air felt good against her skin, and it would keep her awake as she drove. She glanced at the clock on the dashboard—11:06. The sun would be coming up by the time she passed San Francisco. She knew she'd have to stop to rest eventually.

Teresa was within a couple hundred yards of the freeway on-ramp when she spotted the two hitchhikers. They were an interesting couple, even at a quick glance. The guy was dressed entirely in white, and had a head of dazzling blond hair. The girl was thin, pale; her long black hair hung straight to her waist. They stood in the pouring rain without umbrellas. Later, Teresa was to decide that was the reason she had picked them up; ordinarily she didn't stop for hitchhikers. In fact, she'd never stopped before.

Teresa slowed and pulled over to the side of the road about thirty feet beyond them. The guy hurried up to the car, a long green garment bag in his hands. Teresa leaned over and rolled down the passenger-side window. He poked his head inside.

"Can we have a ride?" he asked.

"Sure," she said.

"Where are you heading?"

"North."

"Good." The guy stood back and called to his partner. "Let's go!"

The girl walked slowly toward the car. She had on white pants and a smart black leather coat, which the rain had to be destroying. Her black boots went almost to her knees. She was cute, the guy was, too. Teresa was surprised such a handsome couple would be so down on their luck that they'd have to hitch in the middle of a rainy night. They looked a couple years older than Teresa, who was eighteen.

"Hurry," the guy called.

"I'm coming," the girl answered.

The guy stuck his head inside the car window again. "Can I put this bag in the back?" he asked.

3

"Sure," Teresa said, glancing in the rearview mirror. She didn't want to get rear ended while doing her good deed for the night. Fortunately, traffic was light. The rain had kept everyone indoors. "Do you want to throw it in the trunk?" she asked as the guy opened the back door.

"No," he said. The girl had reached the car, and the guy looked at her. "Do you want to sit in the back with the bag?" he asked.

"Do I have a choice?" the girl asked.

The guy grinned. "You always have a choice."

The girl glanced at Teresa, what she could see of her with the rain blowing through the open passenger window. "I'll sit in back," the girl said flatly.

The two got in. The guy rolled up his window as Teresa pulled away from the curb and then drove onto the freeway. The speed limit was fifty-five; she always did ten miles over and never got a ticket. She glanced over at the guy. He was watching her.

"Hi," she said. "I'm Teresa."

He offered his hand. "Pleased to meet you. I'm Freedom Jack."

She shook his hand. It was as cold and wet as the night. "Is that your real name?" she asked.

"It's what my mother calls me. But you can call me Free if you'd like." He gestured over his shoulder. The girl had chosen to sit directly behind Teresa, which made Teresa uneasy. "This is my pal, Poppy Corn."

Teresa frowned. "Pardon?"

"Poppy Corn," the girl said.

"That's your real name?" Teresa asked.

"It's what my father calls me," the girl said.

"But you can call her Poppy," Free said cheerfully.

4

"You can call her anything you like, Poppy doesn't care. She doesn't care about anything. Ain't that right, Poppy?"

"I suppose," Poppy said. She tapped Teresa on the shoulder. "Can I smoke?"

"Yeah," Teresa said reluctantly. She hated cigarette smoke. "Do you mind if I keep my window down partway?"

"It's your car, you can do what you want," Free said.

"The cold doesn't bother me," Poppy said.

"But the smoke bugs me," Free said easily.

"That's your problem," Poppy said.

"But you want to make it Teresa's problem, too," Free said.

"I don't care, really," Teresa said.

In the backseat Poppy lit her cigarette and blew the smoke at the back of Teresa's head. She turned and looked out the window. "Where are we heading?" she asked.

"North," Free said quickly. "Just the way we wanted to go."

"What's your final destination?" Teresa asked. She wondered what their relationship was—they didn't seem to like each other.

"We have a gig in the Bay Area," Free said. "We have to be there tomorrow. We'd be there now if Poppy hadn't driven our car into a telephone pole. Ain't that right, Poppy?"

Poppy took another drag on her cigarette. "I don't remember a telephone pole."

Free laughed. "That's just my point. You didn't see the damn thing until it was too late."

"What's your gig?" Teresa asked.

"I'm a magician," Free said. "We're booked into the Bard's Club. Ever heard of it?"

"It sounds familiar," Teresa said, lying. "Are you a magician, too, Poppy?"

Free laughed. "She's my prop. I saw her in two, make her float in the air. Tomorrow I'm going to make her disappear. You should see our show. I can get you free tickets."

"It sounds like fun," Teresa said. Maybe San Francisco would be far enough north to make Bill feel she'd vanished from the face of the earth. There might be advantages to staying in the country.

"We're also hoping to visit our parents on the way up," Free said. "I'm going to see my mom and Poppy wants to see her father—why, I don't know. The guy never has anything interesting to say."

"Where does your father live, Poppy?" Teresa asked.

"On the other side of the redwoods," Poppy replied.

Teresa assumed she meant her dad lived just north of Big Sur. "What does he do for a living?" Teresa asked.

Poppy coughed on her smoke. "He's a priest."

"Oh," Teresa muttered. The girl was weird.

"Hey, would you like to see some magic?" Free asked.

"Now?" Teresa asked. "While I'm driving?"

"Sure," Free said. "You can drive and be amazed at the same time."

"Maybe later would be better," she said.

"Now is always the best time." He disagreed and reached into the pocket of his white coat to pull out a pack of playing cards. He handed it to her. "This is an ordinary deck."

"I'll have to take your word for it," Teresa said, fumbling with the deck as she tried to keep her eye on the road. Free was kind of pushy, but she was enjoying his company. He took her mind off all the garbage she had gone through lately. She wished Poppy would quit blowing smoke on the back of her head. She would have to take a shower to get the smell out of her hair. "Do you want me to take a card?" she asked Free.

"I want you to take four cards," he said. "Pluck them randomly from the deck. Don't look at the four you've taken. Put the cards on your lap—facedown—and give the deck back to me. You really should check that you are holding a regular deck first."

It was hard to do what he was asking with just one hand. "I'll be lucky to get four cards out," she muttered, straining in the dark car. She took a couple from near the top and a couple from close to the bottom. She set them between her legs and gave the deck back to Free, who immediately stuffed it into his pocket without looking at it. "Now what?" she asked.

"I'm going to tell you what cards you have between your legs," Free said.

"Sounds suggestive," Poppy said, bored.

Free turned around. "Do you know what the cards are?" he asked.

"They're all jokers," Poppy said.

"You're wrong," Free said pleasantly enough. "You're always wrong." He turned back around. "Do you know what the cards are, Teresa?"

"You told me not to look at them," Teresa said.

Free smiled. He was handsome in a boyish sort of

7

way. She believed his eyes were blue, but couldn't be sure in the gloom. "I was wondering if you had any intuitive feeling as to what you are holding," Free said.

"I'm not the psychic type," Teresa said.

"I am," Free said. "I'm super psychic." He put his hand to his forehead and closed his eyes. "Hmmm. I see aces. I see an ace of hearts. Hmmm. I see an ace of diamonds. I see more. I see the ace of clubs and the ace of spades." He opened his eyes and peered at her. "This is amazing—you drew four aces from a perfectly normal deck of cards."

Teresa laughed. "I don't believe it." She picked up the cards and fingered through them. Aces, one and all. "I don't believe it! How did you do that?"

Free took back his cards. "Magic," he said.

"No, really? Can't you tell me?"

Free shook his head. "If I tell you all my secrets I'll lose my aura of mystery. Ain't that true, Poppy?"

"You lost it long ago, Jack," Poppy said.

"Don't call me that," Free said.

"Free," Teresa said. "Can I examine that deck now?"

"Sure," Free said. He took the deck out of his pocket and handed it to her. Teresa gave him a sly look.

"How do I know this is the same deck?" she asked.

"You don't," Free said. "I have deep pockets. But I told you to study the deck before I did my trick."

Teresa gave a quick glance at the cards. They looked perfectly normal. She gave them back to Free. "Where did you learn your trade?" she asked.

"In the school of hard knocks," Free said. "Hey, are

8

you hungry? I'm hungry. Can we stop? Nothing fancy, you understand. I wouldn't mind a box of doughnuts and a carton of milk from a mini-mart. Would that be all right, Teresa?"

"I don't mind. We'll have to get off the freeway."

"We can always get back on," Free said.

They stopped at a Stop 'N' Go just off the freeway. Two rows of gasoline pumps stood outside. They were the only customers. Teresa and Free got out, but Poppy was comfortable in the backseat. Free paused to ask if she wanted anything. The rain was still coming down, but not so hard. It hadn't rained long enough, though. The air still tasted dirty.

"A carton of cigarettes," Poppy said.

Free snorted. "Those things will kill you."

"The world is filled with things that can kill you," Poppy said. "Get me Marlboros."

"Do you want anything to eat?" Free asked.

"No," Poppy said.

Teresa and Free entered the store and she got her first really good look at him. He was six foot, maybe six one. His white coat sported shoulder pads, but underneath the coat he was strong enough, more wiry than muscle bound probably. She wondered if she had been off on his age. His skin wasn't so smooth in the light of the store; he was older than she had first guessed. His eyes were definitely blue, piercing in their almost white paleness. She suspected his blond hair had been bleached; the roots were darker than the ends. He did have a cool walk, and she could see him on stage as a magician. He almost floated as he moved. Right now he was headed straight for the beer.

"What do you want?" he asked. "My treat."

"I was just going to get a candy bar or something." She was a sugar freak, more specifically a Junior Mints addict. She ate several boxes a day and her body was none the worse for them, except for an occasional pimple, which, fortunately, she didn't happen to have at the moment. She was five six, thin with great legs and clear skin. Her breasts were on the small side, but fit her well. Her brown hair was light enough that she passed as a blond in the summer. Overall her face was pretty enough, in a natural California fashion. Yet the bruiselike circles under her eyes betrayed her recent traumas.

Her lips were lush. She smiled a lot, too much; the smile was more a nervous reflex than an expression of joy. Her blue eyes were clear skies; her dark eyebrows clouds on the horizon. Her nose was a shade too big for her face, and it kept her from being truly beautiful. She had considered having it fixed, but then decided she didn't need to be beautiful. Of course, that was a lie. She occasionally told them to herself, just small ones, white lies that didn't do anybody any harm. The truth was she would have given a great deal to have been irresistible. Then Bill would have still wanted her.

But who cares? I don't care. I wouldn't take him back if he came begging on his knees.

Tiny white lies.

"Do you drink beer?" Free asked. He opened the cooler door and pulled out a six-pack of Budweiser.

"Not when I'm driving," Teresa said.

"I appreciate you stopping and giving us a ride."

"Had you been standing out there long?"

"Nah, not too long," Free said.

"Did Poppy really crash your car into a telephone pole?"

"It might have been a tree. All I know is it was tall and hard and the car looked like hell after hitting it."

Teresa giggled. "You're crazy. Do you know that?"

Free reached for another six-pack. "The later it gets, the crazier I get. Are we going to drive all night?"

Teresa paused. She had never actually invited them to stay with her all the way up the coast. Yet she couldn't see dropping them off in the middle of nowhere, especially if they were all still headed in the same direction.

"I planned on it," she said finally, rubbing her left wrist with her right hand. A dull ache throbbed through it—she must have banged it on something just before she left the apartment.

"Are you all right?" Free asked.

"I'm fine."

"Good." Free carried a six-pack in each hand. "Good."

Teresa picked up two boxes of Junior Mints and a bottle of Coke and brought them to the counter. Free was having trouble buying his beer—the man behind the counter, a short Hispanic fellow of about forty, wanted I.D. Free felt around in his pockets but couldn't find his license.

"What's the matter?" Free asked the guy. "You don't think I'm twenty-one?"

"I need to see I.D.," the guy said.

"Give me a carton of Marlboros," Free said as he pulled a wad of mangled bills from his pocket. The cashier reached behind him for the cigarettes and set the carton down beside the beer and Free's other goodies: a box of chocolate doughnuts, a half gallon of milk, and a bag of potato chips. "How much is it?" Free asked.

"I can tell you how much it is without the beer," the guy said.

Free was annoyed. "I lost my license. Does that make me a criminal? Look at me. Do I look like a kid? Ring up the beer, man, now. We've got a long way to go tonight."

"I need to see I.D.," the man repeated.

"You can't see what I don't have," Free said, defiant.

"Free," Teresa said timidly. "This isn't worth the hassle."

Free looked at her and smiled. All the tension seemed to go out of him in an instant, which made her relax as well. "You're right, babe," he said. "We shouldn't drink and drive." He turned back to the guy. "Ring it up any way you want, man."

They left the store a minute later, without the beer. In the car they handed Poppy her cigarettes. She accepted them with a soft thank-you. Free leaned over and checked the gas gauge as Teresa turned the key to start the car.

"We should get gas," Free said.

"I have three-quarters of a tank," Teresa said.

"We might as well top it off while we're here," Free said, getting back out. "Pull up to the pumps. Stay in the car. I'll take care of everything."

Teresa did as she was told. Free disappeared inside. Behind Teresa, Poppy lit another cigarette. Teresa adjusted her rearview mirror so she could get a better look at the girl. Poppy didn't have a problem with her nose being too big. She was beautiful with big gray eyes and creamy white skin. She was extremely pale, it was true, but her coloring made her look ethereal. With her mane of black hair and her black leather coat she was halfway to being a vampire at a masquerade ball. She, too, looked tired. As she leaned her head back against the seat, Teresa watched the orange light of her cigarette glow in the center of her dark eyes.

"Are you satisfied?" Poppy asked.

"I don't understand," Teresa said.

"You're checking me out. I don't mind. You're the one who's giving us the ride. Do you like what you see?"

"You're a pretty girl, Poppy."

"So are you, Teresa."

"No, I'm not. I'm just OK."

"Why do you say that?" Poppy asked.

"Because it's true."

"You don't say it because you want me to disagree with you?"

Teresa trembled. "No. Why do you say that?"

Poppy was already losing interest. "Because I'm an amateur shrink. Does my smoking bother you?"

"I told you, I don't mind."

"I wish I could quit."

"Why don't you?" Teresa asked.

"It's too late."

"Does your father live near Big Sur?"

"Yeah," Poppy said. "He lives in a big old church."

"You were joking when you said he was a priest, weren't you?"

"Nope."

"Do you really want to see him on the way up?"

Teresa asked. "The reason I ask is we'll definitely have to take the coast road then and it will take us longer. But I don't mind. I was thinking of going that way anyway."

"Do you want to see him?" Poppy asked.

Teresa chuckled. "Why would I want to see a priest?"

"He could listen to your confession."

Teresa shivered, although she still felt hot. Her shirt was damp with perspiration. "I have nothing to confess," she said.

Poppy closed her eyes. "We all have something to confess." She took a drag on her cigarette and coughed. "Some bloody thing."

Free reappeared a minute later. Teresa was surprised to see he had the two six-packs of beer with him. He explained that he had found his license. He set the alcohol on the front seat and casually topped off the gas tank. Then they were back on the road, back on the freeway. Heading north, with no clear destination in mind.

CHAPTER 2

THEY DIDN'T REACH THE COAST UNTIL AN HOUR AND A half later, after they had driven through Ventura. On the drive up Free drank four beers, Poppy two, and Teresa one. Closing on Santa Barbara, the black Pacific on their left, they finished the last of the doughnuts and milk. Finally the air tasted fresh and salty. Free dazzled Teresa with more card tricks and was in a jolly mood the whole time. He did one trick where he had Teresa name a card and then—he said he definitely used magic this time—made it appear in the back pocket of her pants. Try as Teresa might, she couldn't figure out how he had done it.

"I could have made it show up in your underwear," Free said as he took the card back and slipped it into one of his deep pockets.

"I'm beginning to believe it," Teresa said, blushing. She was easily embarrassed when it came to talking about sexual matters, particularly with a cute guy. She had begun to like Free—his outrageous charm, the pleasure he took in everything she said, his exaggerated displeasure with everything Poppy did. Of course, Poppy didn't say or do much of anything, except smoke and stare out the window at the rain-washed night. Teresa almost wished that Free had been hitchhiking alone. She didn't actively dislike Poppy, not really—the girl just had problems that Teresa couldn't deal with.

Free fidgeted in his seat. He simply couldn't sit still. "So, what are we going to do next?" he asked.

"Do you want to listen to the radio?" Teresa asked. She loved to crank the music up while she drove and drown out her thoughts. But so far they hadn't turned on the radio once. Free brushed aside her suggestion.

"I'm not into canned entertainment," he said. "I need something live, something that's got guts. Hey, I know what! Let's tell stories."

Teresa frowned. "What kind of stories?"

"Ghost stories," Free said. "Horror stories. Real life stories. Anything, I don't care. Poppy and I do this all the time while we're on the road. It helps pass the time. Doesn't it, Poppy?"

"The time always passes without our help," Poppy said.

Free turned around. "You're in a lousy mood tonight. You should be the one to start. Come on, Poppy Corn, tell us the story of your life. Tell us how you became a big star."

"I would rather hear a story I haven't heard before," Poppy said.

Free raised an eyebrow. "Such as?"

"I would like to hear Teresa Chafey's story," Poppy said.

16

Teresa giggled uneasily. "I don't know any stories."

"No," Free said. "Poppy wants to hear the story of your life."

"I'm eighteen years old," Teresa said. "It would take all night to tell you everything that's happened to me."

"We have all night," Poppy said.

"Don't pressure the girl," Free snapped. He spoke to Teresa gently. "Why don't you tell us what's going on in your life?"

"How do you know anything's going on?" Teresa asked.

Free shrugged. "You haven't told us where you're going, and why you're going there in the middle of the night. Poppy and I've got the impression you're running away from home. I mean, if you are, that's cool. I mean who wants to live at home when you can be out on the road? But, hey, we're like everybody else. We're curious, we're nosy. We want to hear the dirt. Did you kill somebody or something?"

Teresa laughed. She laughed so hard she almost steered the car off the road. Only Freedom Jack could have asked such a serious question and made it sound so trivial.

"No," Teresa said when she had calmed down enough to speak. "I didn't kill anybody. I wish I had, though."

"Who?" Free asked.

"This guy," Teresa said. "This jerk I know."

"Who?" Poppy asked from the backseat.

Teresa hesitated and felt a lump rise in her throat. She continued to feel hot. Maybe she was getting sick. Maybe she just needed to unburden herself. These two—they were strangers and they would talk on the way up the coast, maybe even become casual friends. But then they'd go their separate ways and never see one another again. Who better to confide in?

She decided right then to tell them about Bill.

The awful thing he had done to her.

"His name was Bill Clark," Teresa said. "He was my boyfriend."

"Why do you wish you'd killed him?" Free asked.

"I have my reasons," Teresa said.

They met at the mall during Christmas vacation. The place was packed because it was only two days before the big holiday. Teresa was there with her mother trying to finish up some last-minute shopping. Actually, even though they were at the mall together and had come in the same car, they weren't shopping as a happy mother daughter twosome. Teresa couldn't buy anything with her mother present because her mother inevitably told her how stupid she was being. Her mother didn't approve of anything she did, which caused Teresa to keep a low profile in her presence. Her mother didn't even like how she studied, lying on her bed and listening to music. And here she was a straight A student and everything.

For the moment, thankfully, Teresa was alone to make her own decisions. She was hungry and stopped at the food section, which was huge, the selection vast. She could have Mexican, Italian, Chinese, or American. She ended up at a Carl's Jr.—she liked the charbroiled chicken sandwiches. She had to get in a long line. After a minute or two the guy in front of her turned around and his hands were also laden with bags. He had brown hair and brown eyes, a nice build. He also had dimples; she noticed those first. She always liked dimples on a guy; they made any one look less dangerous. She hadn't dated much and guys still scared her a little. This one was about her age.

"It looks like it's going to be a long wait," the guy said.

Teresa nodded. "At least fifteen minutes just to put our orders in."

He nodded at her bags. "Do you have something for everybody?"

She smiled. "No. I ran out of money. I'm going to have a lot of people mad at me this year." Actually, that wasn't true. She had bought something for everyone who might conceivably expect a present. It had broken her to do so. She had spent over four hundred dollars. She'd make it back, though, she told herself. She gave guitar and piano lessons every day after school. She had been playing both instruments since she was nine and was considered very good. She also sang and wrote songs, although only a few people knew that. Her best friend, Rene Le Roe, was one. She had spent a hundred dollars on a cashmere sweater from Nordstroms for Rene.

"You can't please everybody," the guy said.

"Ain't that the truth," she said. She was always trying to please people and thought it was because she was a nice person. Although sometimes she did worry that she just wanted people to like her. She knew those weren't exactly the same things.

"Are you here by yourself?" the guy asked.

"My mom's around somewhere. We're supposed to meet in Waldenbooks in an hour. How about you?"

"I came by myself. Do you know what you're getting for Christmas?"

It was an interesting question, she thought. "I know my parents are getting me a new guitar because I had to help them pick it out. My brother—he lives in San Diego—he'll probably give me a gift certificate for clothes. He always does. My best friend will get me something totally off the wall. Something I'll never be able to use or even show anybody."

"How about your boyfriend?" the guy asked. The question was probing—the fact didn't escape Teresa. But the guy asked it so easily that she didn't know if he was interested in her. She didn't even know if she wanted him to be.

Lowering her head shyly, she muttered, "I don't have a boyfriend."

"Then I should buy you lunch."

She raised her head quickly. "Pardon?"

"Can I buy you lunch?"

"Why? I mean, I don't even know your name."

"I'm Bill Clark. Who are you?"

"Teresa."

"May I buy you lunch, Teresa?"

She felt her cheeks redden. "Can I order anything I want?"

Bill smiled, showing his dimples. "Anything you desire."

They both ordered chicken sandwiches when the time came—half an hour later. By then Teresa knew that Bill was a senior in high school like herself and that he was interested in astronomy and physics and that he wanted to journey to Mars before he was forty. By then she also knew she wanted to go out with him, and when he asked for her number after they'd eaten, she couldn't find a pen quick enough.

He picked her up for their first date two days after Christmas, which was a Saturday. Her parents grilled him for thirty minutes before giving him full responsibility for their darling daughter's very existence on the planet. Bill took it all in stride. When they were in the car he said his mother had died when he was a kid, and that he never saw his dad because the man worked all the time. Teresa felt a pang of sympathy for Bill, yet at the same time she couldn't imagine a more wonderful setup.

They went to dinner, and Bill talked about the Big Bang Theory—the origin of the universe. He said that fifteen billion years earlier all matter in creation had been condensed into a single point of mass as tiny as the period at the end of a sentence. But that this point exploded, and generated trillions of degrees of heat and a great light that still glows faintly to this day. The background radiation of the universe, Bill called it, and it sounded so incredible because the light of the candles on their table was in his eyes and he had shaved and dressed up just for her. When he was through talking she asked him a question.

"Then what are we?" she asked.

"What do you mean?"

"If all matter in all the universe can be condensed into a period doesn't that mean that we're like nothing? Just spirits floating around on a ghost planet?"

Bill nodded. "That's true. All of matter is almost entirely space. Only an infinitesimal part of it is solid."

"Then how come you can't see right through me?" she asked.

He smiled. "Who says I can't? Who says I can't tell exactly what you're thinking right now?"

"What am I thinking?" She didn't even know herself, but it was something about him. Everything about him. He was wonderful, the way he talked about important things—big things. All she had ever thought about was the smallest of things—herself and what others thought of her.

Bill raised his water glass, indicating she was to do the same. They chimed the crystal together. "You're thinking you want to go out with me again," he said.

"I don't know if I can." She enjoyed watching his face fall. "I mean, there's a lot of background radiation around you."

He laughed. "There's a lot of light around you, Teresa."

Later, after a movie neither of them enjoyed, he took her to his place. His father was at work. The man must have made big bucks—the house was gorgeous. Teresa felt nervous. She had never been alone with a guy late at night. But she was excited, too, and she trusted Bill. She knew he wouldn't try to take advantage of her. They sat in the living room beside a huge aquarium of exotic fish. Bill remembered her comment at the mall about getting a new guitar. She hadn't talked about her music over dinner. She'd been too busy forming galaxies and creating planets for alien beings to inhabit. His words had carried her to places she had never been before.

"So have you been using your new guitar?" he asked.

"Of course. I play all the time. I've played every day since I was nine."

Bill was impressed. "You're a real musician?"

She giggled. "I'm not real, remember? Neither are you. Just a bunch of empty space playing with empty space."

"I have some empty space in the next room that looks like an old guitar my dad never learned to play. Would you play it for me?"

She was shocked. "Oh, I couldn't do that. I'm not a performer."

"Then who do you play for?" he asked.

She shrugged. "I just play. I only play for other people when I give lessons."

Bill stood. "Then you can pretend that you're giving me a lesson. I want to hear you."

"Why?"

"Because I know you're going to be wonderful."

He returned a minute later with a guitar that had seen better days. He sat on a chair across from her. The steel strings were rusty, and it took her several minutes to tune the instrument. Bill sat patiently while her heart pounded against her chest. She knew she was good, but she didn't know his tastes. He had said some nice things to her at dinner, but she had no real idea if he liked her the way she liked him.

"What would you like to hear?" she asked finally.

"I can just name any song and you'll know it?"

"I don't know every song, but I know a few."

"Play one of your favorites," he said.

"I want to play one of your favorites."

"Teresa."

"What?"

"Play something that you've composed. And don't tell me you haven't written any music. You have, I can tell."

She was amazed. "How can you tell?"

"Because you're a creator. If you were there at the start of the Big Bang I'm sure you would have done a great job of organizing the universe. Maybe better than whoever did do it."

His remark was ridiculous, of course. But maybe that was why it touched her so. She knew then what she was going to play him. It was a song she had written that morning, while she sat daydreaming about him. She just intended to play him the music, but hardly had she begun to strum the chords than her mouth opened and the words poured out.

"There was a song in my room I wanted you to hear.
It had colors and rhythms and a story most dear.
But I kept it to myself out of sorrow and fear.
That you would hear it too soon and never again come near.

"But you heard it anyway and it made you laugh.
You saw me too soon and your eyes cut me in half.

24

But I laugh, too, and I don't want it to end.
This time together with the boy who gave me
 this painful yen.

"You think I am an interesting stranger.
I have secrets you don't know that could be a
 danger.
I have lies that would hurt me to share.
But truths that could comfort me if you care.

"So why don't I stop now.
Why don't I take my bow.
I can't say with words in a song.
Things that can't be found in time no matter
 how long.
We sit together and talk of everything that
 might go wrong.

"But let's not talk, let's not say.
We can't see where we are, we don't know
 the way.
Let's just say we have today.
We have today.
And if that is enough to keep fate from asking
 us to pay.
Then I will stay beside you until the month
 of May.
I will stay beside you any kind of way.
Boy, this is all I want to say.
Until the month of May."

They sat in silence when she was finished, Bill
staring at her. Her heart was no longer pounding. It

had sunk into a warm glow of golden light at the beginning of a new creation. Bill smiled and shook his head.

"What's it called?" he asked.

"The Month of May."

"It's still December. It's a long way to May."

"Yeah," she said. "I know."

He got up and walked over to sit beside her. He leaned over and kissed her on the lips. It was enough for another hundred songs, a thousand lonely nights. It was the first time she had ever been kissed by a boy and she was glad it was this boy. He let go of her and shook his head once more.

"That was beautiful," he said.

"Thank you."

"When did you write it?"

She hesitated only a moment. "This morning."

He understood. "You're beautiful, Teresa."

"You really think so?"

He nodded, moving to kiss her again. "I think May's just around the corner. I'm not going anywhere if you're not."

He held onto her half the night. Where was there to go?

Nowhere. Every other road led nowhere.

"He just used me," Teresa told Freedom Jack and Poppy Corn as she finished telling them about her first date. "He made me think he cared about me when he didn't."

"Did you guys do it the first night?" Free asked.

"Jack," Poppy complained.

"I told you not to call me that," Free snapped.

"Well, really," Poppy said. "Show some class."

"We didn't sleep together that first night," Teresa said.

"But later, huh?" Free said.

Teresa hesitated. "Sure, yeah. I was happy, I was having a good time." She gestured weakly. "I was a fool."

"The bastard," Free said. "What did he do to you?"

"It's a long story," Teresa said.

"You have to tell us," Free said. Then he became still for a moment—rare for him. "But I suppose it's our turn to talk. What do you say, Poppy?"

"You never stop talking," Poppy said.

"Shut up."

"Gladly."

"You have to tell a story," Free complained. "It's part of the deal we made with Teresa."

Poppy lit another cigarette. "Why don't you start and I can jump in when you get lost."

"It's a deal," Free said. "Let's tell her about John Gerhart and Candice Manville."

"Who are they?" Teresa asked.

"Friends of ours," Free said. "They led an interesting life. We both knew them. They had a kind of Romeo and Juliet romance."

Teresa grimaced. "I hope they didn't commit suicide at the end."

"They were no Romeo and Juliet," Poppy muttered.

"Let me tell you how it went," Free said.

CHAPTER 3

"JOHN AND CANDICE FIRST MET WHEN THEY WERE JU-
niors in high school," Free said. "John had just come
to the L.A. area, where a lot of their story takes place.
He was originally from Detroit. His mom and his
stepdad moved out to L.A. because his stepdad had
been laid off at a GM plant. He was looking for work.
The family didn't have much money. John had to get a
job right away, on top of going to school. He worked at
a gas station doing everything his boss was too lazy to
do. John was great with cars—he could fix anything
that was broken. But he was kind of wild. Sometimes
he broke things that didn't need to be fixed. He was a
cool guy, though, and wasn't going to be a mechanic
all his life. Not with his good grades. He took a lot of
math and hard sciences and knew he'd be an engineer
someday.

"John ran into Candice not long after he started at
his new school. She was a beauty, and John always had
an eye for good women. He called her Candy, al-

28

though she didn't let anyone else call her that. They shared a math class. Candy wasn't the academic type. She liked to read, but mainly she enjoyed sitting and spacing out. She was a dreamer, that Candy. She should have been born on the moon. Anyway, John began to help her with her math before he even asked her out. He knew right from the start he wanted her. He was just biding his time, being cool, and she really needed his help. She had a C that was looking more and more like a D every day.

"Candy needed more than tutoring. John moved so he was sitting behind her, and during tests he would pass her the answers. John was a whiz at math. Candy's grade went from a C to a B in a month. The teacher was out to lunch so they never got caught. Candy would have gotten an A in the class if she hadn't started so far in the hole. John did get an A. He got A's in practically everything.

"Finally John and Candy started dating. He didn't even ask her out. She asked him out! She was hot for him by then. John was hot for her, but he liked a girl bouncing before he jumped—if you know what I mean. They went to the movies, ate, drank beer—the usual teen scene. They went to the beach a lot, too. Candy looked like sex and sun lying in the warm sand. By then they were heavily involved, physically I mean. They did it just about every day. They got along great. Their junior year ended and, of course, they had more free time, although John still had to work hard at the gas station. If he didn't bring home the bacon, his stepdad carved it off his ass with a belt. John had a bastard of a stepdad. The guy had lost a few screws welding on so many bolts for so many years on the assembly lines in Detroit. They couldn't stand the sight of each other.

"But all this time John didn't know that Candy was keeping a secret from him. He didn't find it out until they were already back in school for their senior year. You see, Candy didn't take any art classes. Her parents wanted her to be a doctor. I say her parents and not her because Candy didn't really know what she wanted to do with her life. The one thing she knew was she loved to draw. She was a genius, really, when it came to sketching stuff. But she kept her abilities secret from John because she was afraid he'd make fun of her. That was one thing about John. He couldn't stop teasing people. He would tease a guy pushing himself up a hill in a wheelchair—not because he wanted to hurt the guy's feelings, but because he wanted to get a laugh out of him. John was always trying to get a laugh out of everybody.

"Well, one day he stopped by Candy's house when she didn't expect him. She was up in her room working when he walked in. She had an easel set up by the window with a drawing of John and herself at the beach. She was sketching John then. She was using charcoal—Candy only drew in black. Later she told John it was because she was color-blind, but he thought she was just kidding. A miniscule number of girls are color-blind, John knew.

"Anyway, he walked in on her while she was in the middle of her sketch and she just about died of embarrassment. And Candy didn't embarrass easily. How could she when her brain was always sitting on the goddamn moon? But she was sensitive when it came to her art. She knew John would razz her no end, which was exactly what he did. But I knew John. I knew how he really felt about Candy's work. Her talent blew him away, it really did. The second he saw her drawing of him his jaw dropped. He couldn't believe how much *power* she had put in it. She caught a side of John not many people knew. The strong John. The one who could make things happen. He could have been great.

"But John didn't let his jaw stay dropped. He quickly started in on her, saying that she had made his ears too big and his nose too long and that he should be carrying a rifle and looking macho. Candy couldn't listen. She pulled the sketch down, tore it in two, and threw the pieces in the garbage. She started crying, which just made John hassle her more. There was no point in showing weakness around him. He saw it as an invitation to score more points. John saw all of life that way. That he had to score, to get ahead while the getting was good. Candy was the opposite. She let things happen, and if nothing happened, so much the better. She could bury her head in a book and know the world would keep turning.

"Afterward, though, John felt bad for giving Candy such a hard time. He wanted to see more of her stuff, but she wouldn't show it to him. She took all her sketches and hid them at a girlfriend's house. From then on John never knew what she was drawing. It bugged him. He cared about Candy. He wanted to be involved in all parts of her life. But she wouldn't let him in and that was too bad for her because John could have helped her get ahead, pushed her in the right direction. John could see already that Candy wasn't cut out to be a doctor. She didn't have the discipline. He tried explaining that to her parents, but then they didn't want him coming over so he backed off. John was pragmatic. He wasn't about to give up his girl just to save her vocation.

"The year went on. John got great grades and Candy did well, mainly because John passed her the answers on every test they took. They had arranged their schedules so that they spent almost the entire day sitting beside each other. John and Candy mastered the art of cheating with mirrors, flying spit balls, invisible ink, Morse code, and even telepathy. Yeah, they were so close it was like John just had to look over at Candy and she would know what he was thinking. If the answer to question twenty was C, he would say, 'I can always C you Ms. C. Wherever you go, my eyes can C you.'

"John was possessive of Candy. If she so much as spoke to another guy, she got chewed out. And the other guy would end up with a bloody nose. John had a temper, there was no arguing that. His temper got the worst of him near the end of the school year. At the beginning of June, Candy and John were just a few days shy of graduating. They had one last test to take—chemistry. It was John's strongest subject and Candy's worst. She couldn't pick up a test tube without thinking she was taking an early pregnancy test. She thought the periodic table of elements wasn't square enough. This was the girl who wanted to be a doctor!

"But she was on her way. She had gotten accepted at Berkeley, the same school as John. They had it all planned. They were going to live together in an inexpensive bungalow, get night jobs at a movie theater, and make love at least twice a day. The only reason she got accepted at Berkeley, though, was because John had helped her raise her grades so much her junior and senior years. She was going to a school where she probably didn't belong and John knew it. But he figured he'd be able to pull her through.

"Anyway, they had this one last test to take in chemistry. John was prepared. Between lube jobs at the gas station he had studied his brains out. Candy had spent the same amount of time drawing pictures of God knew what. She walked into the test barely knowing that the formula for water was H_2O. They planned how John would get her the answers before the test began, but they didn't plan enough. By this time they were both cocky, and thought that all teachers were fools. They never thought they'd get caught.

"Their teacher's name was Mr. Sims. He had the habit, during tests, of leaving the classroom to do odd jobs in the storage area. He had done this all year, and John used that time to slip Candy answers. The storage area was directly connected with the classroom, Sims could always pop in at any moment. But John could hear him coming. Near the end of the test, Mr. Sims disappeared into the storage area. Candy was really sweating by then and looking over at John with pleading eyes. She hadn't got past the third problem—there were twenty on the test. John pulled out a piece of scrap paper and jotted down his answers. He was already done with the test. He was always the first one done.

"John decided to drop the answers on Candy's desk

as he went to the front of the classroom to hand in his test. Mr. Sims was nowhere around, he made sure of that. Of course, there were a lot of other people watching. It was a class of forty students. But John didn't think about them much. He couldn't imagine that one of his classmates would turn him in. That was one thing about John. He gave people a hard time, but he didn't mean anybody any harm.

"Maybe it was the stress of the moment. Maybe John had made the girl feel bad earlier in the year and she had just been biding her time to get back at him. It doesn't matter. John crumpled his scrap paper with the answers on it into a ball. As he got up, he let the paper fall on Candy's test paper. Candy was ready, waiting for it. But she didn't have time to get it out of sight before a girl in the back shouted for Mr. Sims to come into the room. Wait, I take that back. Candy did have time to get rid of the evidence. She could have stuffed the ball of paper in her mouth and swallowed it—but she froze. Mr. Sims was back inside in a moment. He wanted to know what was happening. The girl in the back pointed at John and Candy.

"'John just gave Candice all the answers to the test,' the girl whined. She had one of those annoying voices that you just knew would make her future husband want to have extramarital affairs. Mr. Sims hurried over to John and Candy. He was in a sour mood. His wife had recently left him for a filmmaker of animal documentaries. He had been taking it out on his classes by making his tests harder and harder. Still, John didn't expect Mr. Sims to slap him down. After all, he was his best student, the only one in class who was getting an A. He watched as Mr. Sims stormed toward him. He whispered to Candy to make the crib sheet disappear. Maybe Candy didn't hear him.

"'Are you two cheating?' Mr. Sims demanded. He wasn't big—he was short and round. But he had been trying to act bigger since his wife had left him. His face was beet red, and John misjudged how angry he was.

"'No, I was just handing in my test,' John said. 'I don't know what Annie's talking about.' The girl's name wasn't Annie. It was Sally. She had a two-ton chip on her shoulder. She jumped out of her seat and hurried to Mr. Sims. All this time, of course, the cheat sheet had been sitting right in the center of Candy's desk. Sally triumphantly reached down and picked it up and gave it to Mr. Sims.

"'I saw John drop this on Candy's desk a few seconds ago,' she pronounced in her whiny voice.

"'Is that true?' Mr. Sims asked Candy.

"'No,' John said quickly.

"'It's a complete lie,' Candy agreed.

"Mr. Sims wasn't buying it. He would have had to be pretty stupid to do so. 'Then where did this paper come from?' he asked as he unwadded it.

"John was feeling cocky. 'I think it's Annie's,' he said.

"'My name's Sally and you are a big fat liar!' Sally shrieked in her nasal twang.

"'This looks like your handwriting,' Mr. Sims told John when he had the paper open in his hands. 'I dare you to deny it.'

"John shrugged. 'I don't deny it,' he said. 'I just don't think it's that big a deal. Candy didn't have a chance to study on account of her mother being so sick and all. Ain't that right, Candy?'

" 'My mom has been feeling lousy since she grew her tumor,' Candy told Mr. Sims. 'She's up practically every night throwing up blood.'

" 'I saw your mom last month at the grocery store,' Mr. Sims said, turning redder by the minute. 'She looked fine to me.'

" 'You should have asked her out,' John said. 'Her old man's such a pain in the ass—you wouldn't believe it. I think you and Candy's mom would make a nice couple.'

"Mr. Sims practically blew a blood vessel right then. Like I said, he was sensitive about his wife leaving him. And he was smart enough to know John was making a reference to that. He shook the cheat sheet in Candy's face. 'Did you ask John to give you these answers?' he demanded.

"Candy didn't answer right away and only stared at John. Finally John was beginning to see that things were not going to end happily. But he still had no idea how bad it could get. He figured there was no point in both of them getting in trouble. He said to Mr. Sims, 'I gave her the answers. She didn't ask for them. She didn't even know what I was doing when I dropped the paper on her desk.'

"Mr. Sims nodded slowly, staring John hard in the eye. He stuck out his hand. 'Give me your test,' he said. John did as he was told. Then Mr. Sims took the exam and methodically began to tear it into tiny pieces.

"That freaked John out. He had studied hard for that test. It was a big one—it counted for a quarter of his grade. Taking a zero on it would drop his A down to a C. His own temper began to burn, and good things never followed when that happened. 'What the hell did you do that for?' he yelled at Mr. Sims.

"'Because you are a spoiled little cheat,' Mr. Sims yelled back. He pointed toward the door. 'Get out of here and take your filthy mouth with you!'

"'You can't kick me out!' John yelled back.

"Mr. Sims poked an angry finger in John's chest. 'I just did. Get out. You just failed your final exam. You are excused.'

"John slapped his finger away. 'You're pissed because I suggested you go out with Candy's mom,' John said. 'I was just doing you a favor. God knows you're going to have trouble finding another woman looking the way you do.'

"Mr. Sims lost it right then. He poked John in the chest again, hard this time so that John had to take a step back to keep his balance. 'You didn't just fail this test you two-bit cheat,' Mr. Sims said. 'You failed this class. That fancy college you think you're going to won't be taking you after I get through talking to them.'

"John didn't like the sound of that. Mr. Sims was talking about fooling with his future, and John had big plans for his life. He was going far. He was going to do great things and people like Mr. Sims weren't going to stop him. But John hadn't learned yet that the smaller the person, the easier it is to trip over him. Mr. Sims had his leg sticking out and John was running by at the wrong time. John blew his top. He pulled his arm back and clenched his fingers and landed a fist on Mr. Sim's jaw. The teacher hit the floor for a midafternoon nap—minus a few teeth."

"Wow," Teresa said, speaking for the first time. She hadn't even thought to interrupt. Free was a natural storyteller, and as he gathered steam, Teresa felt she was right there with John and Candy.

"John was expelled the next day," Free continued. "In fact, he was arrested on charges of assault. His case went to trial and he got a strict judge. He couldn't afford a lawyer and the one the state appointed him was an alcoholic. He trembled every time John spoke to him—he was worse than useless. Mr. Sims and Sally testified against John. Mr. Sims walked into the courtroom with his whole face bandaged—it was all a show. John was found guilty before he was sworn in. He ended up spending the summer in juvenile hall— not a nice place. He lost more teeth than Mr. Sims had before he saw the sun again as a free man. But John was tough, he survived. He survived by getting even tougher. He didn't have anything left in his life to soften him. He didn't get to see Candy once while he was inside. Her parents wouldn't let her go anywhere near him. Their daughter was going to be a doctor. John Gerhart was already on the road down to nowhere. That's how they saw it. That was how John's own parents saw it. His mother only visited him twice, and that was because she felt guilty.

"While John was doing time, Mr. Sims and the school principal wrote a letter to U.C. Berkeley telling of the incident. They left out how Mr. Sims had poked John in the chest twice before John struck him. They called him a violent young man and stated that his academic achievements were a result of years of cheating. Berkeley wrote John a stern note of rejection. When John finally got out of juvenile hall, he felt he couldn't get into a decent school anywhere."

"What happened to Candy?" Teresa asked.

"Nothing," Free said, smiling. Obviously Free must have known John well to give such a detailed account of his days in high school, but Teresa doubted Free had liked John. Free had told John's story with enthusiasm, yet, oddly, without much personal emotion.

"Did Candy get to go to Berkeley?" Teresa asked.

"Sure," Free said. "In the eyes of the powers that be, she had done nothing wrong. By the time John got out, she was at school, living the happy life of the college coed."

"But didn't John try to find her?" Teresa asked.

Free stared out the window. "Yeah, he tried. But he found her at the wrong time."

"What do you mean?" Teresa asked.

"I should tell this part," Poppy spoke in the backseat. "I knew Candy better than Free did."

Teresa glanced over her shoulder. It was a rare moment; Poppy didn't have a cigarette in her mouth. The quiet girl was leaning to the right, resting against the garment bag Free had shoved in the backseat.

"Tell me what happened," Teresa said.

"I will," Poppy said. "After you tell us more about Bill."

"That's fair," Teresa said. "Bill and I had been going together less than a month when he came up with the idea of making me a singing star. That was the beginning of the end."

CHAPTER 4

IN REALITY BILL AND TERESA HAD BEEN DATING FOR SIX
weeks when Bill set up an audition for her at the
Summit Club in Newport Beach. During those six
weeks they had grown close. It was rare if they didn't
talk at least once a day on the phone. Their favorite
pastime was to go for long walks and ramble on about
everything. Teresa felt that since she had met Bill
more words had come out of her mouth than during
all her previous years combined. She seldom felt shy
around Bill and didn't feel she had to do the right
thing all the time. Bill never criticized her. Being at
ease in his company actually took Teresa some getting
used to. At home with her parents—in particular with
her mom—she could never relax.

Bill surprised her with the idea of auditioning after
they'd been to a late movie. He was kissing her in his
car outside her apartment. She was anxious to get
inside before her dad came out, but at the same time
she was hoping Bill wouldn't stop with simple neck-

ing. Bill didn't come on too strong, and she respected that. But now she wanted a little less respect and a lot more intimacy. She wanted to get closer to him, to love him more, and she didn't know how to do that without having sex with him. But she couldn't tell Bill that because she was too shy and he might not think she was good enough for him. That was the only thing she worried about when she was around Bill—how attractive he thought she was. His repeatedly telling her she was pretty didn't free her from that insecurity. It seemed to heighten it, in fact.

"How would you like to have a bigger audience than me?" he asked, right in the middle of a passionate embrace. She had to pull back a foot to absorb what he had said, and even then she didn't understand it.

"Pardon?" she said.

"I want other people to hear you sing," Bill said.

"Why?"

"What do you mean, why? Because you're great."

"Do I have to be great for everybody? I like being great just to you. What are you talking about, anyway?"

"An audition," Bill said.

"An audition for what?"

"At a club, down by the beach. It's called the Summit. It's a fun place. It has live talent every night. There's an audition this Tuesday afternoon. I think you should go. I'll go with you. You'll blow them away, I guarantee it. It's a paying job, Teresa. You can make more in one night at the Summit than you do giving fifty private lessons."

Teresa sat back. The windows of Bill's car were steamed up. She reached over and cracked her window and took a deep breath of fresh air. "This is the craziest thing I ever heard," she muttered.

"Why?"

"I can't play at a club. I'm not loud. I'm not exciting. I don't dance, and I certainly can't get people up dancing. I play the guitar and piano and sing soft ballads. If I played at a club at night, people would go to sleep."

Bill studied her intently. The light from a distant street lamp cut across his face, making him look like two people at once, neither of whom she knew as well as the guy she had just been kissing.

"The Summit hires all kinds of talent," he said. "They have rock groups, rap groups—they have people who sing ballads. The main thing is they like people who are good. And you're real good."

"I'm in high school," Teresa said.

"That doesn't matter. It's your talent that matters. Your age doesn't count. They'll recognize that, I guarantee it."

She had to chuckle. "You can't guarantee anything, Bill. You're in high school, too."

He stopped. "I've already played them a tape of your stuff."

"What?"

"You heard me," Bill said.

"I don't have a tape of my stuff. I've never taped anything."

"I do. I have."

"What? No. You taped me without my knowledge? How could you?" Her voice was choked with hurt. "How could you do that to me?"

"I didn't do anything *to* you. I did something *for*

43

you. Teresa, you're a wonderful girl, but you lack self-confidence. The only way you're going to get it is by getting out into the big bad world and winning. You can win at this club. I played three of your songs for the owner and he just said, "I want that girl."

"Did you tell him how old I am?"

"I told him you were twenty-three."

"Bill!"

"It doesn't matter! He wants you."

She was close to crying and she didn't want to do that. Not in front of Bill. Crying girls were never attractive. She realized Bill had done what he had out of enthusiasm for her songs. Yet she felt violated. Her music was her secret. She had shared it with Bill, trusting him, and he had gone and told the whole world about it.

"It does matter," she said. "I told you the first night, I'm not a performer. Entertaining people is a lot more than just being able to write music and songs. You have to have style and charisma. I'm not twenty-three. I'm barely eighteen, and I'm as charismatic as a doorknob."

"Not when you close your eyes and sing," Bill said.

"I don't close my eyes when I sing."

Bill laughed. "You always close your eyes when you sing. How do you think I was able to tape you without your knowing it?"

"You shouldn't have done that, you know. I could sue you." She pushed at him. "Stop laughing at me."

"You're so beautiful when you're angry!"

She had to smile. "You've never seen me angry, buster."

He kissed her suddenly, a quick one. "Will you do it?"

"No."

"You have to."

"Why?" she asked.

"Because I want you to. It will mean a lot to me. It'll mean even more to you."

"I'll audition and they'll see I'm just a kid."

"We'll dress you up," Bill said. "You'll look like a woman of the world when you walk in. You'll look like Madonna."

"I don't want to look like Madonna. She can't sing."

"And look how far she got. Will you do it?"

"No."

"That no doesn't sound as strong as the first one. Will you do it?"

"No."

"They're getting weaker."

"My parents won't let me."

"We won't tell them."

"What will we tell them?" she asked.

"That we're running off for a romantic weekend— every weekend."

She stared at him. He was so adorable and cute. She reached out and ran her hand through his hair. It was impossible to stay mad at him.

"Can we?" she asked.

"What?"

"Run away for a romantic weekend?"

He was surprised, but he recovered swiftly. "If you do this for me, Teresa, I'll do anything for you."

She considered, but not for long. "You have a deal, Mr. Bill."

The Summit was bigger than Bill had led Teresa to believe. On a good night two hundred people could crowd in. When she got out of the car with Bill to check the place over, she wanted to faint.

"I can't play here," she said.

"What difference does it matter how big it is?" he asked. "Your eyes will be closed."

He dragged her inside. There were no auditions going on then, just a chubby middle-aged custodian wiping tables up front. He had a cigar in his mouth and sweat dripping off his fat cheeks.

"We're here, Mr. Gracione," Bill called.

"This isn't the owner?" Teresa hissed in Bill's ear.

"One and the same," Bill said.

"Damn."

"What?"

"Damn everything. I want to leave."

"It's too late now," Bill said cheerfully.

"Are you the girl with the voice?" Mr. Gracione asked as he walked over. He had on a wine-colored sports coat and a mine of gold chains around his hairy chest. He looked like a character who had been dug out of a scene from a *Godfather* movie. He stuck out his hand and Teresa felt as if she were being offered a bunch of sausages. Bill and he shook.

"This is the big lady," Bill said. "Teresa, meet Mr. Gracione."

"You look young," he said to Teresa.

"Thank you," she said.

The guy thought that was funny. They weren't

fooling him one bit. "I don't care how old you are. I heard your tape. You really write that song?"

"Which song did you hear?" she asked.

"'Until Then,'" Bill said.

"I wrote it," Teresa told Mr. Gracione, surprised at the pride in her voice. He gestured to the stage at the front of the club.

"Play it for me now," Mr. Gracione said. "Or something else, I don't care. You have your guitar? Good. We won't bother with the mike for now. I'll sit up front. Have you played in clubs before?"

"A few," Teresa said.

"Which ones?" he asked. "You can make up names if you want, I'm not going to check."

Bill mentioned three places in Hollywood that they had agreed upon ahead of time. Mr. Gracione grunted and took a seat. Bill walked her to the stage and left her there. That was the thing about being a performer. Someone could support you totally, be a hundred percent behind you, but when it came down to it you had to do the performing alone. She set her case on the stage and opened it. Her guitar felt strange in her hands—as if she'd never held it before. She was so nervous, and there were only two people in the audience. How would she feel if there was a crowd? This was insane, this wasn't what she was about. Bill was trying to change her overnight, all the time telling her he liked her just the way she was. She turned to Mr. Gracione, prepared to say she couldn't go through with it. The man was smiling at her.

"You got the shakes?" he asked. "Everybody who's any good gets the shakes. If you didn't get them I'd know you didn't care about your music. Teresa, I'm just a guy who owns a club. I'm not a judge for the Grammys. Just sing me a song or two."

His words gave her confidence. "I'll sing you something I wrote last week. It's called 'Warm Summer.'" She stepped up onto the stage and took a seat behind the silent microphone. She sat in shadow; the lights were all off. She strummed a few chords, liking the sound. She had tuned the guitar on the way down to Newport Beach. Clearing her throat once, she began.

"The sweat of the night touches my skin.
I lie on the sheets.
Dreams waiting to begin.
For when, this sin.
I think of you touching my skin.

"But I am not so bold.
I say only this to myself.
Skin waiting so cold.
For me, this gold
Would be having you to hold.

"Warm summer, warm night.
With time you take flight.
Warm summer, cool night.
I miss you.
Do you miss me?
Tonight?

"Days so long.
The sun burns my sky.
Everything seems so wrong.
For me, this sad song.
Is knowing you'll be gone.

"Still, you say, I love you.
Your words sound so fine.
But are they true?
For I, I love you.
I wish we could make this all brand-new.

"Cold winter, cold night.
With time you took flight.
Cold winter, lonely night.
I still miss you.
Do you miss me tonight?
Tonight?"

When she finished no one clapped—she hadn't really been expecting it. But it would have been nice if Mr. Gracione had jumped up and cheered. He only stared at her with an odd expression, and his first question puzzled her.

"Are you two going together?" he asked.

She hesitated. "Yes."

Mr. Gracione glanced at Bill. "But you're getting along fine?"

"Great," Bill said.

Mr. Gracione nodded. "Just wanted to be sure." He grinned. "Teresa, you put such sorrow in your voice you had me worried for a moment. That's an amazing song."

"You liked it?" she asked, sounding as if she were three years old. "Do you want to hear more?"

He stood and clapped his hands together once. He was excited. "I loved it and I want to hear everything you've written. But I can tell you right now you've got a job here, if you want it. You'll have to play Tuesday

49

and Thursday evenings. Traditionally those are quiet nights—both for the number of people we draw and the music we offer. But when you get more experience we might stick you on a Friday or Saturday night, just to see how it goes. On weekends this place cooks. How does that sound?"

Teresa beamed. "Wonderful." She knew she would remember this moment and feeling for a long time. Because it was a feeling she had never experienced before, except perhaps when Bill asked her out the first time. She looked at him from her triumphant place on the stage, and saw how happy he was for her. It was true; he had made it all possible. She couldn't imagine loving him any more than she did right then. "It sounds wonderful," she said.

Her opening night didn't come for another two weeks. The delay was at her request. She wanted to get her act really together and polished. She was surprised to learn that Mr. Gracione didn't mind if she played the same songs twice in the same night—because she was to come on twice. Her set was to last about forty-five minutes. She was to go on at eight o'clock and then again at ten. Mr. Gracione hadn't gone totally out on the limb with her. He still had two other acts playing the same nights she did.

Teresa was delighted to learn that Mr. Gracione was an intelligent and sensitive man, one who was always in an upbeat mood. There was nothing he loved more than owning a place where people could have a good time. He told her, in fact, that it was OK if she bombed her first night out. He wasn't going to drop her because of it.

Strangely enough, or maybe it wasn't so strange, while she got ready for her debut she saw less of Bill. Practicing with him in the room didn't work. They'd end up spending most of the time talking. Also, he frankly didn't know much about music. He'd want her to change a chord on a particular song, or drop a line here or there, or add one that he'd written—his list of changes went on and on. She didn't mind his making suggestions, it was just that they weren't any good. It was hard to tell him that without hurting his feelings, but she managed somehow.

Telling her parents about her job proved the disaster she had anticipated. She broke the news to her father first and hoped he'd help her convince her mother that it was a good thing rather than the end of the world. Her father's reaction was curious—he hardly reacted at all, which somehow hurt more than anything. But her mother was not so impartial. The lines started immediately. Was she out of her mind? Did she think she could just drive to the other side of the city twice a week—in the middle of the night for godsakes—because she wanted to? In the car *they* had given her? Who did she think she was anyway? Madonna? What songs was she going to sing? When had she ever written songs? How come they hadn't known about them? Why was she keeping secrets from them? What other things hadn't she told them? Who had put her to this, anyway? Bill? Of course, it was that Bill. She shouldn't be seeing so much of that guy anyway. He just wanted her for one thing. All guys did.

Jesus.

Yet her mother calmed down when she heard how

much money Teresa could make at the Summit. A percentage of the take, you say? . . . How much is that? . . . Hmmm, sounds like they're taking advantage of you, dear. . . . Well, we'll think about it.

So they let her do it. But she had to buy all her own clothes from now on, they said, and pay for her own gasoline, which she already did.

Then there was Rene Le Roe, Teresa's best friend. Teresa hadn't seen Rene nearly so much since she'd started going with Bill, and now that she was barely seeing Bill she *never* saw Rene. They were curious best friends, as far as best friends went. They had known each other for ages, and before the advent of boyfriends and stardom Teresa had made it a point to talk to Rene at least every other day. Rene went to another school even though she lived only two miles away. Teresa, in fact, could walk to Rene's house.

The depth of their communication, even when they were talking regularly, left something to be desired. What it all boiled down to was that they didn't have much in common, except that they were both shy. Rene knew nothing about music. Teresa knew nothing about horses—Rene's passion. Rene did poorly in school and never studied, while Teresa, of course, excelled in all subjects and spent a good portion of her waking hours studying. It was as if they were best friends because no one else wanted to be friends with them; and that, too, was odd.

Rene was a beautiful girl. Her long black hair was shiny and the color of a winter night sky. Her exquisite face was pale, but not sickly. She looked, rather, like a princess who had waited years alone in a tower room for a prince. Really, that was why Rene had never had a boyfriend. She was picky; she was ready to wait forever. Perhaps they had only become friends so they could wait together.

But Teresa had finally broken free of her tower. She was waiting no longer. She called Rene a week before her scheduled debut. Rene knew about Bill, of course. Teresa had described him to Rene at length, but the two had not yet met. Rene greeted Teresa's news of her romance and her job at the Summit with quiet enthusiasm. Teresa never stopped to consider that Rene might be jealous. Certainly, Rene never gave any sign that she was.

Rene wanted to come to her opening night, and that was fine with Teresa. The more Teresa practiced and the more she talked to Mr. Gracione, the greater her confidence grew. She began to see—not out of arrogance but with a recognition of what was genuinely there—that she had talent. That she could write songs that spoke to people and that she had a voice that touched people deeply. Even her own mother— wonders never cease—burst into her room one evening when she was practicing. Teresa had been singing softly, but apparently her mom had been standing outside the door eavesdropping. Her mom paid her the highest compliment she was capable of by saying, "I can't believe that was you I was listening to."

Her mother and father said they'd come to see her when she was comfortable with her show. Teresa began to notice, as the days went by, a note of pride in their voices when they talked with her about her job. They weren't totally out of touch, she realized.

Finally the big night arrived. Teresa dressed with care, or rather, she tried on everything in her closet and decided nothing would do. Fortunately, she had Rene with her, and the two of them wore the same size. Rene drove her over to her house—or started to at least. The two of them planned on going to the club together. Bill was already at the Summit, making a last-minute equipment check for Teresa. She didn't have a direct pickup on her acoustic guitar and the microphone attached to the main mike was often filled with static. Mr. Gracione had promised her a new mike and Bill was there to make sure it was installed properly.

"Maybe my red dress would look nice under the lights," Rene suggested once they were on the road in Rene's black Miata. Teresa was far too nervous to be behind the wheel of a car.

"I'm sitting on a stool," Teresa said. "I'm leaning toward pants."

"How about my green suit?" Rene said. "You know the one?"

"Yeah. I don't know. Green is such a nature color. This is a nightclub. I think I should wear black."

"Black is so sober."

Teresa nodded. "You're right. How about white?"

"I don't have anything white. You're the one with the white pants suit."

"I am? Where is it?"

"In your closet," Rene said.

"Oh yeah. Did I try it on?"

"No."

"I want to try it on," Teresa said.

"You want to go back home?"

"Yeah. Quick, let's hurry. I'm supposed to go on in two hours!"

Rene laughed softly. "I'm glad it's you and not me," she said as she turned the car around.

"Just don't you and Bill start hooting me as soon as I come out."

Rene nodded. "I won't make a peep." She added, "I'm glad I'm finally getting to meet Bill. Is he really as cute as you've told me?"

Teresa considered. "I think so. But I can't tell anymore. I like him so much I don't even think I can see what he looks like. Do you know what I mean?"

Rene shook her head. "I've never had that experience."

"You will one day soon." Teresa giggled. "Just don't have it tonight with my boyfriend."

Naturally, the white pants suit looked perfect to Teresa—until they were back in Rene's car, heading for the club. But by then Rene wouldn't allow Teresa to change her mind. It was less than ninety minutes to curtain. Teresa had never had a car ride that went so slow. Her nervousness was intolerable. She kept trying to pretend that the show wasn't that night, but her pounding heart and dry throat were not fooled. Again and again she went through everything that could go wrong. Her single worst fear was that she would freeze up and not be able to sing a word. But she also knew if she could just get past the first song, and hear people clap, even one person in the crowd, she would relax. She reached over and touched her best friend on the arm.

"I'm glad you're here with me tonight," she told Rene.

The sentiment in her voice surprised Rene for they didn't normally expose many deep feelings to each other. Rene was reserved—probably always would be. She lived with a father who was a public prosecutor in the district attorney's office downtown, and a stepmom who had never wanted to have children of her own.

"I'm glad you're glad," Rene said. "Are you sweating?"

Teresa clenched and unclenched her hands. "Blood. I don't know why I let myself be talked into this. I hate feeling this way. It's like waiting to be led to the gallows and all the people are watching, waiting to see you fail." She briefly closed her eyes. "If I screw up I know I'll want to die."

"I envy you," Rene said.

Teresa opened her eyes. "You just think you do. I'd give a lot to be able to change places with you right now."

Rene glanced over at Teresa. She had such dark eyes—they almost cast their own shadow. Yet, like her black hair, they were beautiful. "I feel the same way," she said.

"Really?"

Rene nodded. "Really."

"Why?"

"Because you look so alive right now."

"I just told you, I feel like I'm about to die."

Rene was silent for a moment. "A lot of sick people say that when they first heard they were going to die—they really began to live." She shrugged. "I think that's what I was trying to say, maybe not."

Teresa had to laugh. "Do I look that bad?"

Rene smiled sadly. "You look wonderful."

At last they reached the Summit. The parking lot was full. Full! That was impossible. It was Tuesday for godsakes. Mr. Gracione had told her that Tuesday nights usually drew about sixty people. She realized in an instant what had happened. The club owner had been telling his regulars to be sure to stop by for her show. Oh no, she thought, she could alienate his entire clientele in one night. She almost tripped and fell as she got out of Rene's car.

"More people than you expected?" Rene asked.

Teresa swallowed. "Yes."

They went in the back door. Mr. Gracione and Bill welcomed them. Both were dressed in suits. Teresa didn't even know Bill owned a suit. He must have bought it for this evening. She introduced him to Rene and the two shook hands and said things she hardly heard. Her hands were shaking now. She couldn't imagine how she was going to be able to play the guitar. Mr. Gracione took her aside.

"How do you feel?"

"Terrible. The place is full. Why did you invite all these people?"

Mr. Gracione was apologetic. "I've been talking enthusiastically about you. I guess some of my enthusiasm wore off. But don't worry, kid. You'll kill them."

"I suppose it's either me or them," Teresa muttered.

She went alone to the dressing room to try to pull herself together. Outside the brightly lit cubicle she could hear the crowd waiting for the next act. Her guitar was there, sitting on a chair. Trying to tune it, she broke a nail—so low down it began to bleed. It could have been the straw that broke the camel's back. Tears swelled in her eyes and she lowered her head. She could hardly breathe she was so scared.

I can't go on like this.

Then she felt strong hands on the back of her neck, rubbing her tight muscles. She didn't need to look up; she knew Bill's touch. For a minute she just let him massage her, let her stress flow into him. Finally he touched her chin and lifted her face up. She opened her eyes. He was smiling and she was crying and that made her mad. Her anger must have shown on her face because his smile widened.

"This is fun," he said.

"You should be the one who has to go out there." She held up her bleeding finger. "Look at me, I can't play. I can't even tune my stupid guitar." More tears filled her eyes. "I can't do it, Bill."

He sat beside her and put his arm around her. He kissed her cheek. "You can do anything you want, Teresa. Do you know why?"

She sniffed. "Why?"

"Because I love you."

He had never told her that before. A warm balm washed over her. She only wished she had the time to enjoy it. "How does your loving me help me sing?" she asked.

"All you sing about is love. Now you get to sing from experience."

A faint smile touched her lips. "What makes you think I love you, buster?"

"You've been writing all these songs about me," he said.

"I wrote most of my songs before I met you!"

He kissed her again on the cheek. "It doesn't matter. They were about me."

She almost told him then that most of her songs were about lost love. But she didn't because she wanted to hold him instead, and tell him that he was probably right—that she loved him as well.

Mr. Gracione introduced her and she stepped out into the lights. The lights—they were so bright she could have been set down before the gaze of a star. But she supposed that was why so many people wanted to be stars—so that many eyes would always be on them. Yet, with the blinding glare, she could hardly see anyone more than a few feet from the stage. She heard their welcome cheers, however, and the few scattered gasps. It was her age that brought the latter, she knew. She sat on her high stool and cradled her guitar on her lap.

"Thank you," she said. "This is the first time I've ever sung in public. I want this first song to be for Bill. It's called 'Until Then.'"

She closed her eyes.

It was true—she always did close her eyes when she sang.

> "Fill the sails and fill the space,
> That lingers in your night.
> Hear the songs the echo sings,
> And see the stars take flight.

"When the night decides to show the day,
We'll sail away,
Far away,
Until then.

"Take me back to nowhere and lay me by
   your side.
And talk of things that you've seen in your
   dreams.
A laughing wind, a sunlit smile, a broken sky
   to mend.
A distant shore,
Till there's no more.
No message left to send.

"When the night decides to show the day,
We'll sail away,
Far away,
Until then."

Teresa stopped and opened her eyes. She saw nothing but bright blinding light and heard nothing but silence. Silence can be kind when you're waiting for the sound of acceptance. Because the longer the silence after a song, sometimes the louder the applause. Such was the case this time. When the clapping came, it broke over her like a loud wave of joy. They clapped for a full minute, and then they began to cheer. What could she do except laugh? She heard her giggles through the P.A. system and she sounded so young it made her laugh even harder. It was the greatest moment of her life, really—there had been a few of them lately. She hoped there'd be plenty more.

I love you, too, Bill.

Teresa didn't get together with her friends until after her second show. Between acts Mr. Gracione occupied most of her time—telling her that Madonna had better move over. It was hard to tell who was more excited—him or her. He presented her with a bouquet of red roses in the dressing room and gave her a big bear hug even as her hands continued to tremble. She broke another nail tuning her guitar for the second set, but she didn't care. How strange it was, she thought, to go from paralyzing fear to rapture in only an hour. She would never have imagined her emotions could swing so far so fast.

Her second show went even better than the first. She didn't repeat any of her material, and from what she could see, most of the crowd stayed to listen to her again. They cheered so loudly after her final song that she knew her ears would still be ringing the next day.

Bill and Rene finally caught up with her in the dressing room. Before leaving the club, she quickly called her parents. They amazed her. When she asked if she could come home later than she had told them, they said fine. They sounded happy for her. They said they were going to her very next show—on Thursday.

The three of them went to an all-night coffee shop that overlooked the ocean. For Teresa it was a dream. She actually pinched herself, half expecting to wake up. Bill was as giddy as she was. Only Rene seemed to have retained a semblance of normality, but she was smiling far more than usual and Teresa knew she was excited for her. They ordered Cokes and coffee and a *whole* chocolate cake.

"Bring us half a gallon of vanilla ice cream while you're at it," Bill told the waitress, handing back the menus. He added, when the waitress was gone, "I should have asked for candles."

"They don't have candles in a coffee shop," Teresa said. "Besides, it isn't my birthday."

"But it is," Bill said. He lifted his glass of water, indicating they were to have a toast. "You were reborn tonight. When I saw you up there under the lights, everybody's eyes on you, I knew you had at last emerged from your cocoon." He swirled the ice around in his water. "To the new Teresa Chafey! May she live long and prosper!"

"Do we have to bury the old Teresa Chafey so soon?" Teresa asked, laughing. "She wasn't such a bad sort. She managed to catch Mr. Bill, after all."

Bill turned to Rene. "Do I look like a caught man?" he asked.

Rene lost her smile for a moment as she stared at Bill. Her smile returned and she slowly lowered her head. "You look like a guy who does what he wants to do," she muttered.

Teresa giggled. "Hey, he can do what he wants as long as he does it with me!"

Rene seemed embarrassed, which surprised Teresa. They were all just carrying on, after all. Briefly, she wondered what Bill and Rene had talked about between her acts.

"I was just kidding," Rene said.

There was an awkward pause. "I was just kidding,"

Teresa said. She glanced at Bill. "Am I missing something here?"

"No," Bill said quickly. "What are you talking about?"

"Nothing." Teresa smiled. "Nothing." She reached over and took Bill's hand. "So, I fulfilled my part of the bargain. Now it's your turn."

Bill blinked. "What?"

"Our romantic weekend," Teresa said. "You said we could go on one after I was a superstar."

Bill hesitated. "Sure. We'll have to do that sometime."

"Not *sometime,*" Teresa said. "Sometime soon."

Bill shrugged. "OK."

"How can you go away for a whole weekend?" Rene asked. "Your parents won't let you—you know that."

"I've gone away for the weekend with you," Teresa said. "Remember that time we went down to San Diego together? I'll tell them I'm going away with you again."

Rene was doubtful. "Your mom would probably call my mom to see if we were really together."

"I guess you'll have to come with us, then," Bill said to Rene.

Rene blushed again. "All right by me."

"Hold on a second," Teresa said, forcing herself to laugh this time. "We can work it out better than that!"

Bill was enjoying the scenario. "I think I could handle two girls at once."

Rene caught his eye. She wasn't blushing now. "Don't fool yourself, Bill. There's no way you could handle both of us at once."

"Yeah," Teresa agreed, although the word sounded

hollow in her ears. There was something wrong with this conversation, but she wasn't sure what. The possibility that Rene liked Bill, and vice versa, in a romantic way, never crossed her mind. Why should it? They had just met, and Bill already had a girlfriend. A girlfriend he loved.

Bill drove her home. Rene followed in her car. Rene honked as she made the turn that took her toward her own house. Bill laughed and honked back.

"It was great that Rene could make it to your opening night," Bill said.

"I was happy to have her there," Teresa agreed.

"She's coming Thursday."

"What?"

"She's coming on Thursday."

"I heard you. Why is she coming? I mean, so soon?"

Bill shrugged. "She wants to. Don't you want her to?"

"Yeah. Sure."

"She's fun to talk to."

"Yeah."

They turned into her apartment complex. Bill parked his car next to hers, but he didn't turn off the engine. He leaned over and gave her a quick kiss on the lips.

"You were fabulous tonight," he said.

"Thank you." She ran her hand through his hair, her favorite pastime in the whole world. "Thanks for everything. I'd never have had a night like this if it weren't for you."

Bill squeezed her shoulder. "It's late. You should get to bed."

"Do you want to tuck me in?" she asked.

"I don't think your parents would appreciate that."

"Bill?"

"What?"

"Turn off the car. What's your hurry to leave? I want you to kiss me."

Bill silenced the car and kissed her. But maybe she was pressing the issue. It was late; he must have been tired. He kissed her as if his mind was somewhere else. She was the one to break their embrace, though. She took his right ear in her left hand and massaged it gently, which she knew he enjoyed.

"We would have fun if we went away together," she said.

His eyes were sleepy. "What would we do?"

"Make passionate love."

He chuckled. "Seriously."

"I am serious." She pinched his ear when he didn't show the pleasant surprise she expected. "Come on! Don't you want to?"

He seemed confused. "Sure. We'd have to be careful, you know. I wouldn't want you to get pregnant."

She grinned. "Well, I don't want to get pregnant either. But I've read that there are steps you can take to avoid that." She paused. "Am I coming on too strong?"

"No."

"Then what's the matter?"

"I'm tired is all. I have to get up and go to school in five hours."

"I have to go to school, too," she snapped. "And I've done a lot more this evening than you."

"Teresa."

"I'm sorry, I shouldn't have said that." Inexplicably, in the midst of her euphoria, she felt her heart sink. It was fine to be a star, but she wanted to be desired. "Did you mean it?" she asked.

"Did I mean what?"

"That you love me?"

He sounded irritated—rare for him. "I wouldn't have said it if I didn't mean it. Look, Teresa, let's talk in the morning. I'm getting a headache."

She opened the car door, suddenly feeling small. "OK. I love you, Bill. This is a night I'll always remember."

"I'm sure we'll both remember it," he said.

"He was already in love with Rene," Teresa told Freedom Jack and Poppy Corn. "From that point on he was just trying to figure out how to dump me."

"He still wanted to screw you, though, didn't he?" Free asked. "I bet you he got his fill before dumping you. Am I right or am I right?"

Teresa hesitated and then lied. "You got it, mister."

"It sounds like they liked each other from the start," Poppy said.

Free turned. "You're insensitive, did you know that? Here Teresa opens her heart to us and you're rooting for the other guy."

Poppy wasn't fazed. She never acted as if she was. Not so long as she had a cigarette in her mouth. The inside of the car was as smoky as a barn on fire. Teresa rolled her window down. She had put it up so that they could hear her tale of woe better.

"He doesn't sound like that bad a guy," Poppy said.

"You just didn't know him," Teresa said. "He was a user."

Poppy took a deep drag. "We're all users."

"Candy sure used John," Free said.

"Hah," Poppy told him.

Free turned around once more. "How can you say that? You knew those two as well as I did. Once Candy was where she wanted to be, she never thought about John again. She dumped him like bad luggage. Just the way, I suppose, Bill dumped Teresa."

"There are always two sides to every story," Poppy said.

"Why don't you tell us Candy's side," Free said.

"Where are we?" Poppy asked, as if it mattered.

"Thirty miles south of San Luis Obispo," Teresa said.

"How are you feeling, Teresa?" Poppy asked.

"Fine," Teresa said. She was not being absolutely honest. Her fever persisted. She must be catching a virus, she thought. Her skin felt clammy.

She found it odd Poppy was inquiring after her health.

Poppy sighed. "All right, I'll tell you about Candy. If you get bored just let me know. Her life wasn't all that exciting."

CHAPTER 5

"CANDY DIDN'T GO OFF TO BERKELEY WHEN JOHN WAS thrown in juvenile hall, not right away," Poppy said. "That was June, the beginning of summer. Candy had three months of loneliness to ponder what had happened to John. She felt awful about it, and she thought she was largely to blame. She thought if she had only eaten the cheat sheet as soon as that silly Sally had called for Mr. Sims, the whole fiasco could have been avoided. But then, at other times she wondered if that was true. She had known of John's temper from the beginning, and almost, at the start of their relationship, she had backed away from him because of it. John really couldn't control himself when he got mad. His first reaction was to swing out with his fists. Yet he had never once come close to hitting Candy, which was probably why she had stayed with him as long as she had. But sometimes Candy saw the incident with Mr. Sims as something inevitable. If John hadn't hit a teacher in high school, he probably would have hit one in college. John had taken so much physical abuse from his stepfather, it was as if he had to get back at someone.

"Candy tried the best she could to see John while he was in juvenile hall. But her parents were way ahead of her. They spoke to the people in charge there, and Candy couldn't even get past the front gate. They didn't want their darling daughter associating with such scum. What a laugh. They were so excited about Candy getting into a good college that they had no idea it was all because of John. Candy tried to tell them that, but they wouldn't listen.

"September finally arrived and it was time for Candy to head north to Berkeley. John wasn't sentenced to three months, but fifteen weeks in juvenile hall. So he didn't get out until Candy had been at school for three weeks. John didn't go home when he was released. Candy tried reaching him there and his parents said they didn't know where he was. She left messages for him to call her. Maybe John's parents didn't give those messages to John, or maybe John did get them and was too mad to call Candy. But the result was the same. Candy couldn't get ahold of John and she had to get on with her life.

"She was a mess. She missed John terribly. The more time that went by, the worse she felt. They had been together almost two years. John was the only boyfriend she had ever had. Certainly, he wasn't the kind of guy who was easy to replace. He had a temper, he was arrogant and tactless. But there was nobody with a bigger heart than John. He had worshipped Candy and would do anything for her. There was a lot of stuff between them that Free didn't tell you about. Like the time John took her to the high school prom.

He didn't rent a limo and tux and show up at her door with a corsage in his hand. He got hold of a cement truck, and rented a clown's costume instead of a tux. He made a crown out of tinfoil for her and sprayed it gold so that Candy was prom queen the moment she walked in the door. Now that may sound embarrassing, but Candy loved it. They were the center of attention the whole night. And afterward John fixed a bunch of potholes in the back entrance to the school. He really was a clown.

"But it was John, and not Candy, who stopped them from getting together again after he got out of juvenile hall. And I don't care what Free says—that's the truth. Candy quickly started to drown at Berkeley. Do you know what a premed major requires? Tons of chemistry, physics, calculus, biology—not to mention the usual basic requirements. Candy was flunking out after the first month. Her classmates were way ahead of her from the word go. They had taken preparatory courses in high school. Candy had taken the same courses, but she had never done the work. She hired a bunch of tutors to help her, but they didn't know where to start with her. They'd ask her things like, You don't know what a derivative is? . . . You don't know what an acid base reaction is? . . . You don't know what F equals MA means? Candy began to overload. Maybe she could have sat down and figured things out, if given more time. She wasn't stupid. She just had never developed good study habits. All the stress made her freeze up. Plus she had no interest in the subjects she was taking. Free said it right when he said Candy's parents wanted her to become a doctor. Candy wanted to be an artist, and in her entire schedule, just as in high school, she didn't have one art class.

"The first semester Candy had to drop her hard classes so that she wouldn't have to take F's in them. She ended up with only six credits. She got C's in both psychology and English. Her counselor called her into his office, and it was all she could do to keep him from calling her parents. She promised to do better. The counselor put her on a much easier schedule and told her to forget about going to med school—she would never get in. In a way she was relieved, but at the same time she was in shock. Her parents were paying for her tuition. If they found out the way things were going, they'd be furious. She figured they would probably cut her off. Then what? She would have to crawl home on her hands and knees and get a job at the local fast food joint. Panicking, she went to the administration building and managed to have her parents' address changed to a P.O. box that didn't exist.

"Candy returned home for Christmas and gave vague answers about how she was doing. Her parents fell for it, for the time being. She spent most of her vacation trying to track down John. She went to his parents' house but they wouldn't even let her in the door. All she got was John's stepdad. He said he had no idea where John was. She went to his old job—same story. Her leads were in short supply. John had never been one to have friends. Really, that was the sad thing about John. She was his only true friend, and he had so many wonderful qualities, but people couldn't see beyond his abrasive personality. But what was equally true was that John had been Candy's only true friend. When they had lost each other, they lost a great deal. Candy returned to Berkeley with a heavy heart.

"She did better her second semester. It would have been hard for her to do worse. But she had no major and was basically a young woman going through the motions of getting an education. She was in a paranoid state. The ax was going to fall soon, she knew. When it did, she didn't want it to cut her whole head off. When her parents found out she was no longer premed, she, at least, wanted to be able to point out that she was still fulfilling her basic requirements. For that reason, she was afraid to take an art class. It was absurd. Sometimes she'd stop by a drawing class to see the quality of work being done by the students. I wouldn't be exaggerating to say she was better than the teachers. Candy had talent, and it was all going to waste.

"Near the end of the second semester she met a man. She wasn't looking for a relationship, although she was desperately lonely. It was just one of those things that happened. The relationship was cursed. The man was a teacher, and he was a *married* teacher, in his midthirties. His name was Henry and he taught art. He saw some of her work—she showed it to him in a brave moment after talking to him. He fell for her because she was a natural genius and he was an academic hack. That's what he told her. But maybe he fell for her because he was as lonely as she was.

"He wasn't a bad man, Henry. He was a patient teacher. His students loved him. He just didn't have any talent, and his wife was always nagging him to quit teaching and get a commercial job where she thought he'd make more money, but where he knew he would fail miserably. He wasn't handsome at all, not like John. In fact, he was the opposite of John in every respect. He was so mild mannered that he had a hard time protecting his place in line at the movies. He wore thick glasses and was helpless without them. He had an ulcer and was always chewing Maalox tablets.

"But he was a comfort to Candy. He took her to dinner and helped her with her homework. But their relationship had severe limits placed on it. He wasn't ready to leave his wife—he told her that right at the start. And the administration couldn't find out about their affair or he'd lose his job. They went to late dinners, late movies, and he always wore a hat. Henry's wife didn't seem to care. She was having her own affair with a building contractor.

"You might think Candy was a fool to get involved with such a man and I don't think that Candy would have argued with you. Her eyes were open. She knew where her affair was headed, which was nowhere. But she liked Henry, she really did. She may even have loved him, although not in the same way she had loved John. In her heart she had decided she was never going to love anyone as much as she loved John.

"Strangely enough, the whole time Candy was with Henry, she drew very little. For one thing, if it was risky for her to take art classes before, it was doubly risky now. Henry couldn't be seen with her on campus. Then there was the difference in their abilities. It was her talent that had caught his eye but when he was away from class, he later explained, he liked to forget drawing. Sure, he would comment on a drawing if she showed it to him. He would offer constructive criticism—things to do to improve. Yet he really did not encourage her. Maybe he was jealous. Maybe he was just trying to spare her a dead-end career. Berkeley had more starving artists than any other city in the world.

"Summer break came. Candy stayed in Berkeley. She had tasted freedom and she didn't want to have to live under her parents' roof anymore. She got a job at a department store and one as a waitress—just to make ends meet. Her parents refused to send her money as long as she wasn't taking classes. But she felt she needed a break from studying. She had managed to complete the second semester with a C average and hadn't dropped any more classes. She continued to see Henry. His wife went to Europe for the summer and she saw him more than ever. She even slept at his house a few times. Henry didn't have any kids. He didn't think he ever wanted them. They were careful —they thought—and never had sex without using a condom. But condoms need to fail only once to fail altogether.

"Candy got pregnant. School had restarted and Henry's wife was back in town by the time Candy found out. She waited two months before telling Henry, or even checking for sure that she was expecting. She was in a classic denial mode. It couldn't be happening to her, she thought. It would go away. She would wake up one morning and there wouldn't be a fetus growing in her womb. But she wasn't stupid. She'd had a lot of experience with denial. She was a master at it, and knew all the signs. Finally she went to the campus doctor and had the bad news confirmed.

"Candy told Henry while they were eating popcorn

in the middle of a science-fiction movie about an alien spaceship that was really a part of the mind of God come to visit Earth to save everyone, even the wicked. Candy never did find out how the movie ended. Henry led her by the hand out of the theater and asked her to please repeat what she had just said. He had heard her right the first time, the poor guy.

"Henry wanted her to have an abortion. She agreed that would probably be best. He offered to pay for it, and she said OK to that, too. She didn't have much money. He even offered to take her to the clinic. No, she replied. Too many people might see. Her thoughts were in chaos. She wasn't trying to deceive Henry. She wanted to think about things a little more. But she didn't tell him that. She just said she'd take care of things.

"Candy took the next day off school and went to San Francisco—to the Golden Gate Bridge. For a long time she stood on the bridge with the boats passing beneath her and enjoyed the breeze lifting her hair and the salty tang of the ocean in her nose. She didn't know why she had chosen that particular place to make such an important decision. Nothing happened on the bridge that helped her make up her mind. She received no sign from God. But when she stepped off the bridge she was clear about what she had to do. She felt it deep inside—an absolute conviction that she had to keep her baby. It was good her mind was so clearly made up. Else she couldn't have endured what was to follow.

"Henry got mad when he heard of her decision. He spent hours trying to get her to change her mind. She was too young to be a mother. She had to finish school. He was too old to be a dad. He would get fired if the truth came out. Candy reassured him as best she could. You see, she wasn't asking anything from him. He didn't have to give her a thing, she said. He didn't have to acknowledge to anyone that the child was his. Henry listened to her as she tried to explain why she *needed* to keep the child, but since she didn't even know why, she didn't get very far. But where was there to go? She wanted the baby and he didn't. Their relationship ended that night, although neither of them admitted it for another month. By then Candy was seeing Henry seldom. She didn't see him at all when she began to show in a big way.

"Candy's child was born on Valentine's Day—a small dark-haired baby boy of five pounds six ounces. She named him John, but always called him Johnny. Neither Henry nor her parents were present at the birth. They weren't to blame. Candy gave birth to Johnny in a hospital in a small town on the Oregon coast. She had moved there to get away from it all and to try to start over. By this time she had dropped out of school and gone onto welfare. In a sense her life was in ruins. She had no degree, no money, no man. But Johnny was born healthy and beautiful, and she loved him more than she had ever loved anyone. Or she loved him as much as she had loved John. She always thought of John as the father of the baby, and not Henry. It made no sense, she knew, but that was how she felt."

Poppy Corn fell silent. She reached in her coat and knocked out a cigarette. Coughing, she lit it and took a long drag. She stared out the window at the ocean.

The waves were black foam, rolling toward invisible sand. Teresa kept waiting for her to continue, but the strange girl remained silent.

"Well?" Teresa said finally.

"I'm tired of talking," Poppy said.

"Good," Free said. "I'm tired of listening."

"You're the one who wanted to hear the story," Poppy said.

Free twisted around. He was going to have a stiff neck by the time they arrived where they were going—wherever that was. "I wanted to hear the story minus all the added B.S.," he said.

Poppy tapped her ashes into her palm. Teresa could see the girl in her rearview mirror. "There was no B.S. I just knew her better than you is all."

"You made her out to be a saint," Free said.

Poppy chuckled softly. "Hardly."

"But did Candy ever get back together with John?" Teresa asked. She had really gotten into these characters—despite herself.

"No," Poppy said.

"What?" Teresa grimaced. "You mean they never saw each other again?"

"They saw each other," Poppy said. "A few years later—one more time—on a dark and stormy night. Do you want to tell them about that night, Jack?"

Free was sullen. "No."

"Come on," Poppy taunted.

Free suddenly smiled. Teresa watched him out of the corner of her eye. The smile was a curious affair: mischievous, grim, excited—all rolled into one. He glanced over at Teresa.

"Where did we leave John?" he asked.

"He had just gotten out of juvenile hall and was searching for Candy," Teresa said.

"I didn't tell you he was searching for Candy," Free said seriously.

Teresa stammered. "I—I must have misunderstood you."

Free stared at her a moment more before refocusing on the road in front of them. The endless road—a single broken white line brushed by headlights that showed nothing new. Teresa wondered if she hadn't half hypnotized herself, driving so late at night, listening to this story. No, it wasn't just the story. It was Free and Poppy's voices. They both had such unusual sleepy voices—as if they were related, maybe brother and sister.

"I'll tell you what happened to John when he got out," Free said finally. "I'll tell you the truth. That's all I can do."

CHAPTER 6

"IT'S TRUE WHAT POPPY SAID," FREE BEGAN. "JOHN didn't get out of juvenile hall until after Candy had been at school for three weeks. He didn't call her parents to ask for her phone number because he knew they wouldn't give it to him. He also wasn't sure if he wanted to see Candy right away, and the longer he thought about it the more certain he was. He was mad at her. He had spent hours in juvenile hall thinking about how she had taken it for granted that he was going to help her cheat on her test. She had done so because she was too lazy to study, and because she never thought about his risk. Of course, he hadn't minded helping her until he got caught. But that was just the point—he shouldn't have been caught. She should have swallowed the cheat sheet the second that Annie—or Sally, or whatever her name was—had raised her whiny voice. John had spent an incredible amount of hours thinking about how Candy had frozen at that critical moment. It bugged him, it really did. He only needed her help that one time and she let him down.

"He was also embarrassed to get in touch with her. She was in college, and he was just out of juvenile hall. He wanted to get his life back together before he called her—to show her that he had bounced back after a hard rap. Even though he was mad, he had every intention of seeing her eventually. He missed her more than he could stand, and had spent many nights in juvenile hall remembering them lying together on the beach. Those had been the happiest days of his life.

"John's stepdad lied to Candy when he said that John never came home after getting out. John did go home—for one day. That was all it took for his stepdad to get on his case, calling him a no-good teacher beater and saying he'd never amount to anything. John repaid him by busting his nose. Juvenile hall had not improved his tolerance for abuse. It's hard to stay in someone's house once you've broken his nose. On his first day of freedom, John was out on the streets before the sun even set.

"He didn't have many friends but he had some. He was able to stay at a few guys' houses for a few days. But he had to get a job quick. He didn't want to go back to the garage where he had worked before. He didn't want to do anything he had done before. He wanted to start fresh, stay out of trouble, and make a million dollars so he never had to kiss anybody's ass. At nineteen John was already tired of being pushed around.

"He got a job in a bakery. It wasn't an ordinary mom and pop place. It was the bakery for one of the largest food chains in the western United States. The place was gigantic—several football fields long. You couldn't get within a mile of it and not smell the baking dough. You couldn't work there and not smell like yeast. The place was hot—it felt like it never got below a hundred degrees inside. But the job had advantages. First, it was a union job and the pay was better than at most places. Second, he could work the graveyard shift and have most of his day free to do what he wanted.

"Finally, the job they put him on was easy. The bakery had five machines that sealed various bakery goods in plastic—things like rolls and Danish, stuff like that. John's job was to take the machines apart and clean them. They got clogged pretty quick. The guy who had had the job before John must have been a goof off. The head of the bakery—his name was Tyler—believed that if a guy worked his tail off he could clean all five machines in eight hours. Of course, John was good with machines. He wasn't working at the bakery more than two weeks when he got his job down to three hours. That meant he could take five hours off—if he could stay out of sight—and at the same time give the impression that he was busy with his machines.

"Like I said, the bakery was huge. It had its own shower room, on the upper level. But none of the employees used the showers. The architect who designed the plant didn't realize that when a guy got off work he didn't want to hang around any longer than he had to. He could take a shower as easily at home. John would come on at eleven at night, and by two in the morning he'd have his machines sparkling clean and ready for another day of cinnamon rolls. Then he would head on up to the showers and hide in a stall, reading, listening to tapes, or taking a nap. Sure, occasionally one of the night janitors would find him crashed out. But these guys had no love for the company. They admired a guy who could get his work done and take time off.

"John had it pretty good at the bakery—in the beginning. But things were not going so great outside in the world. He got himself a small apartment in a cheap part of town and that was OK. John never cared where he laid his head as long as there wasn't someone around who was going to wake him up with a kick in the ear. But it was only during this time that John learned to what lengths his chemistry teacher had gone to keep him out of getting into a decent college. See, John figured he would work full-time for a few months, get a little money together, and go off to school. His first choice was the University of San Francisco. He figured he'd be able to see Candy as much as he wanted. Yeah, he hadn't even called her but he was planning how he was going to spend the next four years with her—or however long it took for them to graduate.

"But the university wrote him back a stern letter of rejection. He next applied to U.C. Santa Cruz— again, another school not far from Berkeley. He got the same kind of rejection letter. It made him wonder. He did some investigative work and learned that not only had all the universities in California been contacted by Mr. Sims, but all the state colleges as well. John couldn't believe it. All that was left were a bunch of junior colleges.

"His plans were in ruins. I said he often spent his free time at work goofing off, but he also spent a lot of the time studying the subjects he needed to become an engineer—math, physics, chemistry. He figured he could catch up in no time at all. Now all that was out of the question—at least for the time being. That's the way he thought. Sure, you could say he was overreacting. He could have gone to a junior college and worried about getting into a four-year school when the time came. But he didn't want to do that because he didn't want to have to call Candy at big important Berkeley and tell her that he was taking a few night classes at Cerritos Junior College. I mean, he had his pride and there's nothing wrong with a guy having pride.

"More overtime was offered at work and because John had nothing else to do, he took it. Rather than going in at eleven, he started at six in the evening. He didn't know that Tyler, the head of the bakery and a staunch company man, usually worked to seven or eight. This was the first time the two began to have regular contact. Tyler liked John initially. During the extra hours, he put John on another one of the plushier jobs. John was given a list of what the supermarkets wanted and he'd go around to collect the stuff—forty boxes of doughnuts, fifty boxes of rolls, a hundred loaves of bread, and so on. Then at eleven, with Tyler gone, John would clean his machines and take the rest of the night off. The overtime paid double—he couldn't complain.

"John often took his first break when Tyler was about to leave. Tyler had been a marine, which should have set off warning bells in John's mind right away.

John had never done well with people who were into authority and discipline. But John could be respectful, when it suited him, and Tyler saw in John a kid who'd had a few lousy breaks but who was bouncing back. The two spent a lot of time talking about sports—boxing in particular. John really enjoyed a good fight and boxing was a second religion to Tyler. Tyler, in fact, had boxed in the marines. He was built like a tree stump. John laughingly thought to himself that there was no way he was ever going to take a punch at this guy.

"John didn't get his plush overtime every day. Now and then, the conveyor belts that carried the bread pans away from the oven would break down. When this happened, Tyler would grab whoever was handy and have them manually unload the pans onto racks so that they wouldn't all start piling up. Working right beside the oven was intense—the temperature had to be over a hundred and twenty, maybe a hundred and thirty. The pans themselves were also very hot. When you were put on the hell detail—that's what it was called—you had to wear damp gloves with sleeves attached that reached all the way up to the top of your arms. If you so much as bumped your arm with a pan after taking it off the conveyor belt, it sizzled a nice little black hole in your skin. But the long gloves were a pain. The arm covers were loose and slid down all the time, leaving your arms exposed. The pans didn't even need to touch your skin to cause third degree burns—they radiated so much heat.

"John hated the hell detail with a passion. But Tyler began to use him on it more frequently because the oven belt was breaking down more often and also because John was quick. John could unload the bread pans faster than anybody. At breaks, though, he would have to drink a gallon of water just to keep from getting dehydrated. He began to wonder if the overtime was worth it.

"John was not only quick, he was clever. After working the hell detail a number of times he began to see just how inefficient it was. Men should not be doing what machines could do better, he thought. He examined the conveyor belts and saw that they kept breaking down for a very simple reason. Too much dough was slopping off the sides of the pans as they traveled through the oven. John reasoned that if that slop could be cut down, the conveyor belts would break down only occasionally. He figured a couple of metal scrapers, situated at the receiving end of the oven, would solve the problem. He worked on making them in his free time, late at night, using spare parts. He tried his invention out when no one was around. Invention was too big a word. They were just metal bars, that cleaned and steered the pans as they went by, but as far as John could see, they worked great. He installed them without permission and looked forward to the next day, when he could take credit for his handiwork.

"But John decided, during the night, that he would wait and let his bars do the job before taking credit for them. This they did over the next month—the conveyor belt didn't break down once and there was no need for Tyler to yank people off their usual jobs and put them on the hell detail. The odd thing was, during all this time, nobody asked who installed the new bars. Not even Tyler. John wondered at that, until one evening, when he was having a break, and Tyler was just about to leave for the day. It was then John got another lesson in human nature.

"John was sitting alone in the corner of the break room eating a bag full of fruit. Sandwiches used to be his staple, but since he had begun to smell like the Pillsbury Doughboy he couldn't eat bread or anything with flour in it. John was just about to open his mouth, when Tyler told the workers that *he'd* had the bars installed to scrape the bread pans so the conveyor belts wouldn't jam so often. Tyler puffed up his chest as he spoke. He said he decided to fix the problem himself and be done with it. The men around him nodded appreciatively. A couple even suggested that Tyler should get a patent on the bars, to which Tyler laughed as if that wouldn't be a bad idea.

"It was then John opened his mouth. He said, 'Hey, I was the one who installed those bars. I was the one who figured out what the problem was. What are you talking about?'

"The room fell silent. John had just made Tyler out to be a liar and a braggart at the same time. Some of the men had worked for Tyler for several years and knew how tough he was, and how he didn't like to be embarrassed—ever. They knew John would be fired.

"But John saw none of this. It was just like the time Mr. Sims came striding toward him in chemistry class. John thought he could open his mouth and explain the situation and everything would be all right. But John *made* situations when he opened his mouth, and he had just made a big one. Yet Tyler didn't say anything to John. He just stared through him and left the lunchroom. The rest of the room went back to eating and John finished his apples and didn't give any of it much thought.

"A couple of weeks later John lost his job cleaning the wrapping machines and filling the orders for the individual stores. He was moved onto the hot dog machine. The hot dog machine didn't actually make hot dogs, of course. It was a complicated arrangement of metal fingers and slamming bars that worked to keep the pre-formed dough in the proper grooves in the steel pans so that they could grow into nice bundles of eight connected fluffy hot dog buns. The job was worse in some ways than working beside the oven. It was noisy, and it was dangerous. The operators of the hot dog machine—there were usually two of them at a time—were responsible for keeping the maximum number of buns in the metal grooves. In other words, the people were there to straighten up anything the machine had missed, which was plenty.

"The danger came when you tried to mix metal fingers with human fingers. But that was exactly what the hot dog machine operator had to do his entire shift. He was always darting in and around a pan filled with white dough and steel prongs. It was a good place to lose a finger. John hated the job. He was no fool and knew why he'd been reassigned. Or maybe he was a special kind of fool. He wanted to show up Tyler again—for all the good the first demonstration had done him. He was not working with the hot dog machine a week when he figured out a way to make it more efficient.

"The buns were sticky before they went in the oven, which was natural—they were made of flour and water. It was this stickiness that kept them from resting in the proper grooves. John figured if the buns could be dried just a little before they went into the oven, they would rest happier.

"Next to the hot dog oven was the doughnut oven, which had a row of fans along one side to take off the excess heat. The doughnut oven was always overheating, which was not good—even for an oven. What John did was redirect the conveyor belt that brought in the uncooked hot dog rolls so that they went by the hot air. Then by the time they got to the hot dog machine, they were semi-cooked and much easier for the machine to handle. John did all this work late at night without getting permission from Tyler. He wanted to show the bastard up, make it clear who the inventive genius was. Once again John was able to cannibalize parts. It wasn't much more difficult than setting up a train set.

"Naturally, Tyler immediately knew about the change. John had half expected the jerk to have it torn down right away. But Tyler left the conveyor belt's new turn up long enough to prove its usefulness. John began to think maybe he wasn't such a bad sort, after all. Tyler called John into his office. He started by asking if John was responsible for the reworking of the hot dog roll line, and John said, 'Yeah.' Tyler asked why he had done it, and John quickly explained the logic behind it. In fact, John blabbed on about how it was working great, that it was no longer necessary to have two people work it. Tyler appeared interested. He asked John to accompany him onto the floor and demonstrate how much less attention the machine needed. John thought it was a curious request. It was easy to demonstrate how you had to do something;

hard to show how you didn't have to do it. But John decided to play along. What could it hurt, he thought? The worst Tyler could do was fire him.

"So John lined up at his usual place beside the metal fingers of the hot dog machine, alone, while Tyler and a bunch of others looked on. Soon the pans of blown dry sausages of dough started rolling, and for the first few minutes John didn't have to do anything because all the 'wannabe' buns were sitting easy. But even with John's improvement, there was an occasional bun that sat cockeyed—a bun that the prongs of the machine would miss so that it got burned in the oven. Such a bun came by and John reached out to scoot it into its proper place.

"Now the only thing that made it possible for the operators of the hot dog machine to work so closely with the grabbing metal fingers was that the prongs never touched the pans. They would scrape within two inches of the pan—never closer. An experienced operator could nudge a bun back into place even as a prong was swinging in to get it because the operator knew he had those two inches to work with. Never, never, would he let his fingers stray more than that distance above the pan.

"John was experienced. He had the reflexes of a cat. He knew his exact margin of error. He knew it in his sleep. He knew it blindfolded. He reached out to flick the bun into place just as he looked up and winked at Tyler and his pals. The machine had been on a full ten minutes and this was the first time he had to do anything. He had proven his point. He had the brains, it was obvious. The bakery job was just a stepping stone for him. He was headed for bigger and better things, while a guy like Tyler was going to be in the bakery twenty years from now, still smelling like the Pillsbury Doughboy and still boasting to a bunch of people with cinnamon rolls for brains how he had improved the efficiency of the plant thirty percent.

"But John picked a bad time to look up. His margin of error—those precious two inches—weren't there that day. The metal fingers swept down, and although they didn't scrape the pan, they came mighty close. You might ask, why didn't John notice the prongs were cutting it unnaturally tight? The answer is he should have noticed, but he was too busy gloating about how silly he was making Tyler look. To give him some credit, though, the metal fingers moved in a blur. It was possible he wouldn't have noticed they had been lowered unless the machine had been turned off and each arm was manually swung through its range of motion. John was never to know for sure.

"The metal prong grabbed him. It got hold of his index and middle fingers. At first John felt the catastrophe as nothing more than a hard yank on his *right* hand. He felt little immediate pain—physically that is. But when he looked down, and saw that two of his fingers had been torn off, he almost fainted.

"He went into shock and it was a pity. Because had he been able to keep his wits he probably would have been able to collect his fingers. Then a skilled surgeon could have sewn them back on, and who knows? They might have worked. He might have been able to play guitar with them—piano. Medical science can work wonders. But John was never given that chance. The prongs had grabbed his fingers and stuffed them in with the hot dog buns. They disappeared into the tunnel of the long fiery oven as John's blood gushed onto the floor. John just watched them disappear. The sight of half his hand missing was too much for him.

"The others ran to his aid. Tyler was the first at his side. The man grabbed a small white towel—he seemed to have one ready in his pocket—and wrapped up John's right hand. The towel turned red in an instant. John was bleeding bad. He had lost not only two fingers, but a portion of his actual hand. A big vein was open and squirting. Tyler hurried him to his office, practically carrying him, and an ambulance was called. While waiting for the paramedics, Tyler applied a tourniquet to John's wrist. The bleeding began to slow down. If Tyler hadn't been there, John might have died. In a sense Tyler saved his life. What a swell guy.

"The doctors operated on John for over four hours. He didn't wake up until the next day. His hand was in a cast. It felt as if it was on fire, as if the two fingers that had gone into the oven were still attached, cooking his flesh to cinders. Later he learned that his fingers emerged from the far side of the oven, each wrapped in a fresh hot dog bun. Two women on duty saw them and one of them fainted. Of course, after the fingers were cooked, they weren't worth sewing on.

"John was in the hospital five days and it must have been the third day before he figured out what had happened. Tyler had lowered the metal fingers—it was the only logical explanation. Tyler had disfigured him on purpose, all because John had embarrassed him when Tyler had taken credit for something he hadn't done. John couldn't get over the immense unfairness of it. It was like the incident with Mr. Sims.

He had just been helping his girl get a good grade and he was sent to juvenile hall and barred from a decent college. He had just been trying to improve production at the bakery and now he was crippled for life. John had no illusions about making a full recovery from his injury, although his doctors kept telling him he had to keep a positive mental attitude. 'Does a guillotine victim have to keep a positive mental attitude?' he shouted at them. What did it matter when your head was rolling in the basket. What was gone was gone.

"But John wanted revenge. It was all he could think about. But because he gave it so much thought, he started after it in the right way. He didn't just go after Tyler with a gun. John hired a lawyer when he got out of the hospital, who agreed to help him for a third of the anticipated settlement. That there would be a large settlement seemed likely. John had been hurt at work by a machine that was acknowledged to be dangerous. But John wasn't just after money. He intended to put Tyler in jail. He believed he could prove that Tyler had purposely lowered the metal fingers. He filed two lawsuits, one civil, the other criminal. He asked for a million dollars in damages, a nice round number.

"The matter went to trial, with a judge and jury. The criminal trial came first. The civil trial was supposed to come later, but not too much later. The civil trial would be a mere formality if the criminal trial went well for John. In fact, it would probably be unnecessary. The company would pay up and Tyler would be sent to jail.

"But the judge made a weird decision before the trial began. He agreed to allow John's previous history of teacher beating and juvenile hall time as evidence. It was a ridiculous thing for the judge to do, but more common in those days than now. Naturally Tyler knew of John's past. John had told him about it when they were friends. Who appeared at the trial but the lovable Mr. Sims. John's lawyer, who was as inept as the lawyer who had represented him before he was sent to juvenile hall, couldn't get the court to focus on what had happened to John's hand. He spent most of his time defending John from personal attacks of being violent and paranoid. John didn't help matters by jumping up three times during the trial and screaming at Sims and Tyler. John was found in contempt of court and had to spend a night in jail without his pain medication.

"John had been discharged from the hospital already addicted to morphine and codeine. If he didn't take the drugs, the pain was unbearable. The injury had caused extensive nerve damage—there are an unbelievable number of nerves in the hands. He couldn't sleep without drugs. He couldn't think or even breathe properly. Each time his pills wore off, he'd break into a cold sweat. Just the thought of the pain was enough to terrify him. He was a walking drugstore, a junkie with a doctor's prescription. He felt like an old man and he was only nineteen.

"John lost. Tyler got off. John had plenty of evidence, but he couldn't prove beyond a reasonable doubt that Tyler had lowered the prongs. Certainly, they were in the proper place when the police examined them three days after the accident. John was also hurt by the fact that he had to admit tampering with the machinery without permission. No one cared that his tampering could have saved the company lots of money. It was even insinuated that his adjustment of the conveyor belt had something to do with his losing his fingers.

"When John's lawyer lost the first round, he wasn't interested in pursuing the second. John had to hustle to look for another lawyer, but couldn't find one. The bakery company offered to settle with him—ten thousand dollars if he would just sign a piece of paper—but to John that was a mere pittance. He told them to take a hike. He had been crippled. He'd never be able to hold a normal job again. They owed him a million. They owed him justice. They owed him something for godsakes.

"But all he received was pain. It's a wicked life—the life of constant pain. Some say emotional pain is worse, but those same people usually have nothing physically wrong with them. It was hard to say which was more difficult for John, the days or the nights. Each day it was hard to do the simplest of things—like getting dressed or opening a can or a bottle. Then he had to cope with the fact that he had a deformity that people stared at. That was particularly hard for John because he took pride in his looks. He'd go into a store and people would follow him with their eyes. Even when they weren't following him, he thought they were. If he hadn't been paranoid before, he was now. His self-esteem was wrecked. He couldn't even flirt with a girl anymore. He worried that when he did see Candy again, she'd find him repulsive. He got so he never went outside without bandaging up his right hand, even when he no longer needed the bandages.

"Nights were equally hard. The effect of his pills only lasted three hours at most. He could never sleep the night through without getting up to take something. It was rare when he slept more than three hours. He'd turn over the wrong way and brush his hand and it would be enough to send pain shooting up his arm. Sometimes he didn't even have to move. He'd just lie there and the hand would throb—the severed fingers would, too, and they weren't even there anymore. Talk about phantom pain. John had demon pain. It was as if something had possessed him. He would lie flat on his back at night, sweat, and think about how his life had gone so wrong. That was all he thought about.

"He was on disability for a while but that ran out. Then he was broke. His case against the bakery began to drag on. When they realized he had no legal representation, they withdrew their offer of ten thousand dollars. Now he needed to sue them to get money out of them, but he couldn't afford to sue. He still couldn't find a lawyer. Part of the reason was his temper. He would walk into a lawyer's office and immediately start raving about how unfair the whole world was. The lawyers thought they could never put this guy up on the stand—he would bury himself.

"He tried getting another job but couldn't find one. He had no real skills, except as a mechanic, and with his injury that was out of the question now. He couldn't even work in an office. He couldn't write left-handed, or even open an envelope. But, once more, he was his own worst enemy while he was trying to find new employment. He didn't get a job because he didn't want one. Because he wasn't sleeping right, he was too tired to work. All he really wanted to do was sit around and read and watch TV and take pills.

"He was taking more pills than ever. He had given up on the codeine. Morphine was the only thing that put him in the space he wanted to be in. Ten one-gram pills a day—a lot of opiate flowing through the old veins. The morphine didn't exactly improve his energy level. He would sit most days like a rock, never exercising, and eating only junk food. But he didn't gain weight. On the contrary, he turned into a rail. Nerves can do that, damaged nerves. He went to a pain specialist, who took his last few dollars. All the guy could tell him was that he'd have to learn to live with it. The doctor also thought John was exaggerating when he said how much it hurt. John prayed he could give the pain to someone else, like Sims or Tyler. Had the devil approached him with a deal right then, John would have signed on the dotted line without reading the fine print. He would have done anything to feel normal again.

"If it's a drag being sick or injured, it's doubly bad being broke and sick. John didn't have money to pay his rent or buy groceries. He didn't get aid from a single government agency because he wasn't good at filling out forms, and was worse at waiting for people to get back to him. He was heading for a critical point. Two things converged on him at once. He spent his last dollar just as his personal physician decided it was time he quit taking morphine.

"Now John's doctor was right about one thing. John had become an addict. But his doctor was like the pain specialist. He thought a lot of the reason John took so many pills was because he liked what they did to his head. He refused to renew John's prescription for morphine and only wrote him a prescription for Tylenol and codeine, which was like giving a soldier a BB gun after he'd been used to an M16. John's enemy was pain and now he had nothing to fight it with. Nothing legal.

"John turned to street drugs, and those cost. Until then, he had never stolen a thing in his life. But his situation left him no choice, he thought. He felt robbed of his dignity.

"He sat in his crummy apartment and made plans. He was clever—a good planner. He figured the best way to get money was from inanimate machines that couldn't fight back or identify him. He knew a lot about machines—soda machines, candy machines, cigarette machines—how to get inside them. He bought himself equipment with a bum check: a portable power drill, a crowbar, a set of screwdrivers, and an adjustable wrench. He also got a hammer. Every thief needs a hammer.

"Then began his nights of prowling the streets. In many ways it was better than staying home alone with his pain. When he was doing a job, with the adrenaline pumping, he would actually forget the pain. In those moments, when the quarters came gushing out, he would feel satisfaction, a release from what he had been put through.

"Something else gave him release in those days. Morphine's stronger cousin—heroin. It was hard getting good morphine on the streets, but there was plenty of smack. John waited awhile before trying it, knowing in his heart it might be something he couldn't control, but also knowing the white powder was just waiting for him, like an exotic prostitute, who gave undreamed of pleasure, but who always kept her blade nearby—to insure prompt collection for her services. Ah, heroin, the king of all drugs. At first he just snorted it, and the relief it brought was extraordinary. But soon he was boiling it up in a silver spoon and skin popping it with needles a doctor wouldn't have stored in his black bag. The high was wonderful. For a while John felt as if he had found a true friend.

"Yet even at the start he realized how demanding this friend was. If you didn't give him money, he never visited, and if he stayed away too long it was not only the pain that came, but nausea and cramps—the familiar companions of withdrawal. I said before John was a junkie. Now he was a strung-out criminal. The spiral kept spinning, and for him it could only spin downward. Yet he still had a way to go before he hit bottom."

Free fell silent. Once more Teresa felt disappointed as the tale halted. Still, Free spoke of John as if from a distance, uninvolved. Yet, paradoxically, there was great passion in the choice of words Free used to describe John's adventures. It was as if he were telling the story on two levels simultaneously. One level for each of his listeners, perhaps, Teresa thought.

"I'd like to hear what happened next," Teresa ventured.

Free glanced over at her. "I think we should stop soon, get a bite to eat," he said.

They had been on the road slightly over three hours. She had gasoline left, a quarter of a tank, but it wouldn't be a bad idea to fill up. She wasn't particularly hungry, though.

"Where would you like to stop?" she asked.

"A Seven-Eleven maybe," Poppy said from the backseat. "An AM PM Mart. A Stop 'N' Go." She hadn't made a sound while Free had talked. She hadn't even moved. Free slowly smiled at her suggestion.

"My favorites," he said.

"I don't mind stopping," Teresa said. Free just nodded. She added, "Did John end up back in jail?"

"No," Free said.

"When did he see Candy again?" she asked.

"Poppy told you," Free said. "On a dark and stormy night."

"Was it much later?" Teresa asked.

Free showed impatience. "Much later than what? Than when he started taking heroin? Than when Candy had her baby? Those are all relative events, it's true, but they're not necessarily relative to each other. Time doesn't always move in the same straight line for everybody. When you're in pain time moves real slow. John was in constant pain. Time for him was walking up a steep hill."

"Candy wasn't exactly coasting along on a bicycle," Poppy quipped.

Free turned around. "You're the one who said how happy she was after she had her kid."

"I said how much she loved her little boy," Poppy said. "You can have love and still have plenty of pain. I'd say they usually go together."

Free wasn't interested in continuing the argument.

He turned back to face front and put his hand on Teresa's leg. His fingers were warm now; she felt the warmth through her pant leg. Or maybe it was his electricity entering her body, his magnetism. There was no denying it, sitting beside him, listening to him, she found him more and more attractive. Clearly, he was not romantically involved with Poppy. If he was they had the weirdest relationship she had ever seen. Free smiled at her.

"I want to hear the rest of your story," he said. *"Everything* that happened to you and Bill."

The way he put emphasis on the word *everything* made her uneasy but she rolled with it. It wasn't as if she had anything to be ashamed of, she thought. She had every intention of telling them everything that happened, at least everything she could remember.

But it was only tonight. Of course I can remember tonight.

Teresa reached up and scratched her head, feeling once again how clammy her skin was, how hot she was. It was her illness—that was why her memory was off a little. So she couldn't say exactly what had happened just before she left. It would come to her as she talked, and if it didn't, what was the harm? She had enough facts to convince them that Bill was a bastard and that Rene was a bitch.

"I thought you wanted to eat first," Teresa said.

"I do," Free said. "Then it's your turn to talk. Then we'll stop and visit my mom." He grinned again. "You'll like my mom. She lives in a big stone house by the sea. She can read fortunes."

Teresa laughed. "You believe in that garbage?"

Free laughed with her. "There's so much of it in the

world, how can you not believe in it? But I'm serious, you must ask her to read your fortune so that you'll know what's going to happen next in your life."

"I don't think I want to know," Teresa said.

Free continued to watch her. "They all say that."

Teresa stopped laughing. "Who are they?"

"My mother's clients," Free said. He pointed to the next exit. They had reached the outskirts of San Luis Obispo. After this, if they took the coastal route, the road would narrow and begin to wind as it followed the rugged coast. "Let's get off here," Free said. "This is a good place."

CHAPTER 7

THERE WAS AN AM PM MART NEAR THE OFF RAMP. Teresa stopped in front of the gas pumps and turned off the engine. The three of them climbed out. The rain was still coming down, a light sprinkle. A breeze blew from the direction of the ocean, making her shiver despite her fever. The heels of Poppy's black boots clicked on the pavement as she headed toward the side of the store.

"I have to go to the bathroom," Poppy said.

"I'll go with you," Free said, opening the door to the backseat on his side of the car. "I want to change." He reached inside and unzipped his garment bag. "These damp clothes are beginning to bother me."

"Can I get you anything while I'm inside the store?" Teresa asked.

Free paused and reached inside his pocket to pull out a wad of bills. He motioned her over and thrust two twenties in her hand. "Fill up your tank and get me some beer," he said.

She smiled. "Let's not go through that again. They won't sell me alcohol."

"You can try," Free said, going back to his clothes bag.

"Do you want anything?" Teresa called to Poppy, who was ready to disappear around the side of the building. Poppy didn't turn around.

"Get me a new Bic Lighter," she called.

"But don't you want something to eat?" Teresa asked.

"Peanuts," Poppy shouted.

"Peanuts and popcorn for Poppy Corn," Teresa muttered under her breath as she headed for the front door of the mini-mart. She'd have to pay before she pumped any gas; that's what the sign said.

Inside a frumpy middle-aged woman with a backside as wide across as a barroom TV stood up from her suffering stool and put her Diet Coke down on the counter. "Good morning," she muttered.

"It is morning, isn't it," Teresa said. "What time is it?" She had a watch on but it was easier just to ask.

"One thirty-five," the woman said without checking. Her voice was flat and uninterested in everything. Her brown eyes were equally flat; she might have looked more alive if she'd been lying on the floor with a sheet over her face. Oh well, Teresa thought. It's late.

She headed for the candy section first. Her Junior Mints were all gone. Picking up three more boxes, she moved toward the nuts. There were several kinds of peanuts. She got Poppy a small jar of Planters—the most expensive kind. The beer she didn't bother with at all. Free could buy it himself. He said he'd found his license.

Teresa picked up a carton of milk and a box of doughnuts and stepped up to the counter. There she picked up a lighter. She collected everything with her right hand. Her left wrist was aching even worse than before. The pain seemed to extend up her arm, and the tips of her fingers had gone slightly numb. She studied the area, but could see no bruises, no scrapes —nothing. For the life of her she couldn't remember where she had hurt it.

It was weird. Like the store.

The woman at the counter checked her out with the lethargy of a person twice her age. Teresa handed her one of the twenties.

"I'll get as much gas as there is change," Teresa told the woman.

"That will be eleven fifteen," the woman replied before she had even finished ringing up everything. Teresa was curious.

"How do you know that?" she asked.

The woman stared at her blankly. "How do I know what?"

"How much change I have left for gas. You haven't rung everything up."

The woman slowly bent over and came up with a brown paper bag. "When you've been here as long as me everything costs the same," she said.

The woman never did finish ringing up the order. Teresa left with her bag of junk food and deposited it on her own seat while she got the gasoline pumping into the tank. Poppy Corn and Freedom Jack emerged from the side of the store. They had both changed clothes. Free had donned clothes that were identical to his previous ones as far as cut was concerned, except that these were a kaleidoscope of colors. Poppy had also disposed of her white pants. Now she wore red slacks; the same shade of red as her blouse. Her legs continued to rest snugly in black boots, however, and she kept her black leather jacket on. Free deposited the garment bag in the backseat in the same place as before.

"Did you get the beer?" he asked.

"I can't buy you beer," Teresa said, feeling a bit exasperated. He was fun, but he didn't know when to quit.

"Did you try?" he asked.

"Yes, I tried real hard," Teresa said.

Free glanced at the store. There were posters in the windows; it was hard to see inside. For example, Teresa could no longer see the woman. "I believe you," he said, turning. "I'll be back in a minute."

Poppy touched his arm as he started to leave. Something touched her usually reserved expression. It may have been concern, even pain—it was hard to tell.

"I don't need anything," Poppy told him.

Free appeared surprised at her interest in his actions. But he was as flippant as he always was with her. "I didn't ask you," he said.

"Let's just get out of here," Poppy said.

Free hesitated. He searched her face, and she looked away as he did. She turned to the north and the move could have been an unspoken cue for him to lose interest in what she had to say. He stepped away from her, and her hand fell off his arm, and hung wearily by her side. Poppy looked tired right then, as if the night had finally got late enough to penetrate her silent reserve.

"Get in the car, both of you," Free said. "I won't be long."

The gasoline pump clicked. Teresa withdrew it from the side of her car and screwed the cap back on. Free disappeared inside. She climbed in the front seat as Poppy got in behind her. They sat for a moment without speaking.

"I got your peanuts," Teresa said finally.

"Thank you," Poppy muttered.

"Would you like them now?"

"Maybe later," Poppy said.

"Are you feeling OK?"

"I always feel the same." Poppy paused. "Are you OK?"

"Yes. Well, actually no. I have a bit of a fever. I think I'm catching something."

"There's a lot going around here."

Teresa chuckled. "Do you even know where we are?"

"Yes."

"We're going to hit the winding part of the coast road soon. It's too bad it's not daytime. The scenery is beautiful."

"You've been hot all night," Poppy said suddenly. "You should worry about yourself. Don't worry about me. Can you do that, Teresa?"

Poppy had never used her name before. It had a strong effect on Teresa, an *unreasonably* strong effect. It was as if just by saying her name Poppy had conveyed how much she cared for her, which was really ridiculous when Teresa thought about it. Because Poppy didn't seem to care about anything, except perhaps her friend Candy. Poppy had occasionally showed emotion when she narrated Candy's story.

"What do I have to worry about?" Teresa asked.

"Why are you running away from home?"

"Who said I'm running away from home?"

"I can tell," Poppy said.

"You're wrong."

"Why do you do that?" Poppy asked.

"Why do I do what?"

"Why do you lie?"

Teresa was angry. "I'm not lying. I'm not running away from home. I am going up north to visit an old friend, if it's any business of yours."

"All right," Poppy muttered.

"You don't believe me?"

"No. But what do you care? You know when you're lying and when you're not. It only matters what you know. That's all I'm saying."

"You have some nerve, Poppy, do you know that? Here I go out of my way to pick you up in the middle of the night and take you halfway up the coast and you repay me by giving me a lecture on how screwed up I am. Well, I'm fine. It's you who has the personality problem. Look at you, you can't go two minutes without sticking a cigarette in your mouth. And you just sit in the back making snide comments at Free when he's trying to be friendly. Are you jealous of me or what? Just say it if you are."

"I'm not jealous of you, Teresa," Poppy said.

Teresa suddenly felt as if her balloon had been

deflated. Once more, it was the way Poppy said her name. The girl was insulting, telling her how to behave. Yet when she said her name—it was as if she were her best friend, trying to warn her of danger. There was a warmth in her voice that was hard to identify. Teresa considered a moment before speaking again.

"What's your relationship to Free?" she asked. "Besides being his assistant?"

"Did you get me a lighter?" Poppy asked.

"Yes." Teresa fished it out of the bag and handed it to Poppy. The dark-haired girl lit a cigarette and blew a cloud of smoke. Teresa quickly rolled down the window.

"Have you tried chewing gum?" Teresa asked, coughing.

"I tried everything to quit," Poppy said. "But I've given up trying. You were asking about Jack and me. We used to be involved. We're not involved anymore, at least not romantically."

"Why do you work with him? You don't seem to get along."

"I have to work with him. I have no choice." Poppy added softly, "I care about him."

Teresa hesitated. "Why do you call him by his last name—Jack?"

"It's his name. He doesn't like it."

"I've noticed." Teresa rubbed her hands together and glanced in the store. She could see neither Free nor the woman. "I wonder what's taking him so long," she said.

"He's probably robbing the store," Poppy said.

Teresa chuckled. "He's such an incredible magician, I bet he could do it and no one would notice."

"He knows how to cast a spell," Poppy agreed.

Freedom Jack reappeared a minute later. He walked quickly to the car. He had two six-packs of beer in his hands. He climbed in and set the beer on the floor at his feet. He was sweating and breathing hard.

"Let's get out of here," he said.

Teresa laughed again. "Poppy said you were in there robbing the store. You almost look like you just did."

Free smiled. "Yeah. That's why I put on my psychedelic clothes. It hides the splattered blood." He tapped the dashboard. "Let's hit the road."

Teresa started the car. "You definitely want to go up the coast? The road splits just up ahead. The inland route—highway one oh one—would be faster to San Francisco."

"We've got to see my mom," Free said. "The coast is the only way to get to her."

Teresa nodded. "That's fine with me."

They were back on the highway a minute later. Only then did Free relax in his seat. He opened a beer and offered it to her. Teresa shook her head. He raised it to his lips and took a sip. Poppy sat silently in the backseat, wrapped in clouds of smoke. The rain began to come down again, pelting now. It would be tricky navigating the coast road, Teresa thought, in the dark with the rain quietly thrumming on the roof. She hoped the traffic stayed as light as it was now. She hadn't seen another car in a while.

"Tell us more about Bill and Rene," Free said finally.

"I'd rather hear about John and Candy," Teresa said.

Once more Free reached over and touched her leg, higher this time, above her knee. His fingers squeezed her skin through her pants and he grinned. "You have another Joker in your back pocket," he said.

Teresa blushed. "I do not! When did you put it there?"

"When I pinched your butt," Free said.

Teresa giggled. "You did not pinch my butt. I would have felt that."

"You did feel it." Free let go of her leg and took another drink of his beer. "I can't talk about John until it's my turn. It's your turn now. What happened next? Did you find the two of them together in bed?"

Teresa stopped giggling. She sucked in a painful breath. "Yes."

Free hooted. "I knew it! Tell us what happened." He fidgeted excitedly. "This is going to be good."

"I'll tell you what I know," Teresa said. "But I'm not saying I know everything. They were real sneaky. I told you, Rene said she wanted to come to my second show to see me, but it was just an excuse to see Bill. While I was on stage, and between shows, they had plenty of time to talk and laugh at me."

CHAPTER 8 —

TERESA'S PARENTS CAME TO THE SECOND SHOW, ALONG with Rene and Bill. Having her folks in the audience made Teresa almost as nervous as she had been the first night. The crowd was just as large if not larger. Mr. Gracione said the talk on the streets about her was all good. As she stepped out under the lights, people began to cheer. She felt scared but confident.

Immediately things started to go wrong. On her first song she broke a guitar string. She had done it before, many times while practicing. It was an anticipated difficulty, and she had told herself that if it happened during the show she was just to keep playing and finish the song. But the missing string threw her and she started singing out of tune. She had been on stage two minutes when she ground to a halt and smiled nervously at the audience she couldn't see.

"I broke a string," she said apologetically.

Mr. Gracione brought her a different guitar. She didn't want a *different* guitar—she wanted to have a few minutes to restring her own. It was hard enough playing in front of people, never mind with an unfamiliar instrument. In her dressing room she had an extra set of strings and would have preferred to run to get them. But she didn't want to hurt Mr. Gracione's feelings. The new guitar had steel strings, which she hated; they cut into her fingertips.

She played "Until Then"—the song that had brought down the house two days earlier. Her voice was right on and she played OK, but her mind wasn't focused and she wasn't feeling the song. When she finished, she heard a scattering of applause, but it was nothing compared to Tuesday. Her confidence faltered and she realized how easy it was for a star to become a shooting star and burn out.

The night was far from a disaster, however. Only a few people left after her first set. Most wanted to hear more of her material. That was a good sign. Between acts she restrung her guitar, and the crowd gave her a warm welcome when she reappeared. She introduced a new number she had written that afternoon called "You." It was the best thing she had ever composed and she knew it. She saved it for last. Now she felt like singing.

> "Watched the winter fall over me.
> In a night of dreams.
> Stood under the frosted tree.
> Laugh when I remember how it seemed.

"Thought that we were two.
Called.
You said, who?
Still cry when I think of you.
You.

"My confession is my own.
Saw you kiss me.
Didn't want to go home.
Stood under the barren tree.
Felt the fall come over me.
Felt you.
Who?
You.

"Stay, go—leave me alone.
Stay, leave—I'm asking you please.
Love is the word you say.
But you won't say.
Love.
Please say.
That you'll stay.

"You're so good.
You're so bad.
You came to where I stood.
Made it all seem so sad.
Yeah, I stood under the lonely tree.
Felt the night sink over me.
Lost you.
Why?
Because of you.
You.

"Stay, go—you've stolen my home.
Stay, leave—I'm begging you please.
Love is the word you would never say.
Love.
Please say.
That you'll stay."

The applause was thunderous. She stood up from her stool and raised her arms over her head, as if she had just won a race. Yet she didn't feel so happy as she had a couple of days earlier. The clapping went on for a couple of minutes, but it sounded distant, far away. Something was missing—she didn't know what. Her own voice had chilled even her. She felt as if she had been singing her own sad tale.

Her parents greeted her jubilantly in the dressing room. They brought her flowers. Her father kissed her on the cheek and told her he wanted her to practice in the living room so he could hear. It meant a lot to her—having their approval.

Still—it wasn't the same.

It was late. Her parents wanted her to go straight home. She rode back to her apartment with Bill, but they had Rene with them so they didn't really get to talk. Well, Rene and Bill talked enough. The two seemed to be getting along fabulously. Teresa just sat and listened. Her throat was sore from singing. She was going to have to build up her vocal cords.

It surprised Teresa how little they talked about her show on the way back. She had thought that was the reason they had come. Oh well, she wasn't completely stupid and life sure was full of surprises. So they liked each other—that was fine. They were both good people and they were both still her friends. They could be friends, she wanted them to be. But that was all. She needed another male to add to this trio to fix it, she thought. When they reached Rene's place, Teresa suggested they go out on a double date that Saturday night. Rene, of course, blushed and said she didn't have anyone to go out with her. Teresa just smiled.

"I have someone for you, don't worry," she said.

Bill drove her home, told her how wonderful she had been, gave her a quick good night kiss, and said he was tired and had to get to bed.

"Love you," she said in her hoarse voice, getting out of his car.

"I love you, too, Teresa," he replied.

Her date for Rene was Alfred Morrell. Everyone at school called him "Alf." He was a football player and not a particularly intelligent or personable fellow. Not really Rene's type, but someone who wanted to meet her, and a handsome enough guy. Teresa had him for a lab partner in biology and she had talked up Rene to him even before Rene had shown an interest in Bill. Now she gave him a hard sales pitch. Rene was the most beautiful girl in the area. She was painfully lonely, horny as hell. He just had to meet her Saturday night. Alf said fine, he was agreeable.

Bill wasn't wild about the idea of doubling, but she told him it meant a lot to Rene. He surprised her by saying he didn't think she wanted to meet Alf.

"How do you know who she wants to meet?" Teresa asked him. "You don't know Alf and you hardly know Rene."

"It never works trying to fix people up," he said. "They either meet and find each other or they don't meet at all. You can't make it happen."

Teresa just stared at him. "I disagree. I think they'll get along wonderfully."

They had that conversation on Friday. Saturday morning, eight hours before the big double date, Teresa called a high-priced hotel in San Diego called the Retreat. Nestled in trees beside the ocean, it boasted a five-star rating and two hundred and fifty rooms with balconies overlooking the water. She had heard her parents' friends talking about it. Teresa didn't have a credit card of her own and the hotel didn't want to accept a reservation for the following weekend without one.

"What if I send you a check for the cost of the room for two nights?" Teresa asked. "It'll clear before we get there."

The reservation clerk checked with the manager and was given the OK to save her a room. Excited, Teresa hung up the phone and immediately ran out to mail the check. She had plenty in her account. Mr. Gracione had stayed true to his word and given her twenty percent of the door receipts for Tuesday and Thursday evenings.

Her mind was consumed with fantasies. Bill and she could drive down to San Diego the next Friday after school, have dinner and take in a movie, maybe even a local play. They could swim in the hotel pool and relax in the Jacuzzi. Then—the big night. She would finally sleep with the guy she loved. Which reminded her, she had to take some precautions. Her career was just beginning. Who knows, in a few months she might be touring with a band. She couldn't get pregnant.

Teresa didn't know much about contraceptives. She understood most young couples used condoms, but had heard that guys didn't particularly like them. Not all the alternatives were open to her, not on such short notice. She didn't have time to get a prescription for the pill, even if she knew a doctor who would give it to her. At the library she consulted a couple of women's magazines that contained articles on contraceptives. The sponge seemed her best bet, although it wasn't rated the safest. But her chances of getting pregnant, so she reasoned, would be slim.

She purchased a box of sponges in a drugstore on the other side of town. The pharmacist didn't ask her for I.D., although she was silly enough to think he might. Next time, she thought, Bill could get the contraceptives.

Teresa didn't know where to go to get a book on the art of making love. She had never heard of the kids at school talking about a text that told you what to do. Honestly, she wondered if it could be that complicated that you needed instructions. She wondered if Bill was a virgin, too. She had never thought about it before, although she assumed he was. But for all she knew he had been with lots of girls. He could even have AIDS.

My boyfriend cannot have AIDS.

Bill picked Teresa and Rene up at Teresa's place. Rene had come over earlier. Then they went to Alf's house to get him. He was dressed nicely; she had told him Rene was impressed by class. Alf was in an upbeat mood. They had reservations at a restaurant that had the best steaks in the area and Alf was a meat and potatoes man. Of course, he appeared happy to meet Rene. The only problem was Bill, who seemed kind of grumpy. Teresa thought his disposition would improve as the night went on.

Teresa did most of the talking at first, but she was still slightly hoarse from Thursday night. They got their table at the restaurant and Alf did his best to join in the conversation. But the only thing he knew about was sports, and he was in the company of bookworms. Bill brought up astronomy but Alf made the mistake of asking him if the sun burned as bright when it was on the other side of the earth. Bill didn't respond; he just stared at Alf, who didn't know enough to know how little he knew. Rene spent most of the time with her gaze lowered. Teresa didn't know what to do. It looked as if Alf and Rene were not soulmates.

It was on the way to the movie that the trouble started. Bill made an illegal U-turn and a police car, its rooftop light pulsing red, was on his tail in a minute. Bill swore and pulled over to the side of the road. The police officer got out and wrote Bill a ticket, without listening to a word of his excuse, which did sound pretty lame. Bill was still swearing as they started toward the movie theater again.

"The police force in this town is made up of a bunch of losers," Bill said. "People who can't get jobs anywhere else become cops."

"They do the best they can," Alf said.

"What was that?" Bill asked. He was, naturally, sitting in the front seat with Teresa. Alf and Rene were in the back, although not sitting together. They were pressed up against the side doors so hard anyone would have guessed the car was about to catch fire and they wanted to bail out.

"Not all cops are losers," Alf said.

"And I suppose I deserved that ticket?" Bill asked.

"The sign said no U-turn," Alf said.

"What sign?" Bill asked. "I didn't see any sign."

"There was a sign, Bill," Teresa said as gently as she could. "You just missed it. It's no big deal."

"How come you're taking his side?" Bill asked her. "Since when do you like cops? You told me you hated cops."

"I don't hate cops," she said, which was true, although what he said was also true. Bill had been with her once when she had been pulled over and given a warning slip to get a taillight fixed. She wanted to get off the subject, though, as smoothly as possible because . . .

"My father's a police officer," Alf said quietly.

Bill was stumped for a moment. "W-well," he stammered. "I'm sure your dad wouldn't have given me a ticket for such a minor infraction."

"I don't know," Alf said.

"What do you know?" Bill asked. When Alf didn't answer, Bill continued, "You don't know much about astronomy, that's for sure. What interests you anyway, Alf? Besides football?"

"I like basketball and baseball," Alf said.

Bill barely suppressed a snicker. "That's great, that's wonderful. What do you think of that, Rene?"

"I don't care much for sports except horseback riding," Rene said.

Alf was interested, or trying to be. "You have a horse?" he asked.

"Two," Rene said. "I go riding almost every day."

"That's neat," Alf said. "You don't want to make a left up here, Bill. You'll get another ticket."

Bill suddenly pulled over to the side of the road. He turned off the engine and closed his eyes for a moment. Teresa touched his arm, but didn't say anything. She had never seen him upset before. He took a couple of deep breaths before opening his eyes.

"Rene," he said. "Are you having fun?"

"I'm all right," Rene murmured.

"Are you having fun, Alf?" Bill asked.

"I'd like to," Alf said. "But I seem to be annoying you, which makes me uncomfortable."

Bill nodded. "You are annoying me and it isn't your fault. It's my fault, but I don't think it's going to go away. Why don't we cancel the idea of this double date?"

"Bill," Teresa said. "Give it a chance."

He shook his head. "I can give it more of a chance by getting out of the way as soon as possible." He restarted the car. "Don't argue with me about this, Teresa. I'll drive back to your place. If Rene and Alf want to continue their date, they can go in Rene's car."

"All right," Teresa said, exasperated.

They went their separate ways in the apartment parking lot. Rene and Alf were going to continue on to the movies, but Teresa wasn't sure if she should. Her parents had gone away for the weekend and she invited Bill inside. Perhaps she'd get to try out the box of goodies she'd bought sooner than anticipated. She

120

put on the coffeepot; Bill usually enjoyed a strong black cup. He lay down on the floor in the living room and crossed one arm over his face. She lay down beside him.

"What's bothering you?" she asked.

"Those two couldn't be more opposite," he said.

"Sometimes opposites attract. Look at us. You're a boring intellectual. I'm a swinging rock star." She tapped his chest with her fingertips. "But you're here with me now and I'm glad."

"I was a real pain in the ass tonight."

"You were," she said.

"You don't have to agree with me so quickly."

She leaned over and kissed his lips. "You were wonderful tonight, so gallant, so dashing. I felt myself swoon in your company. I thought, I must be alone with this man. I must take him south next weekend, to a retreat by the ocean, where I can ravage his manly body for two whole days." She paused. "I made reservations for two at the Retreat."

Bill was hardly listening. "What's that?"

"A hotel in San Diego. We're going there next weekend."

Bill sat up. "What?"

"Don't look so enthusiastic."

"I don't know what you're talking about, Teresa."

"Our romantic weekend. Remember? The one you promised? I want to go next Saturday and Sunday. I've already sent in a deposit for the room. We're going to have a great time."

"What about my job? I have to work next weekend."

"Call in sick," she said. "They won't care."

"Says who? Teresa, you can't just make plans without asking me first. It's like doubling tonight. I didn't want to do it. Rene didn't want to do it."

"How do you know she didn't?" Teresa asked.

"Because she told me she didn't, that's how."

Teresa chewed on her lower lip. "I didn't know she had your phone number."

"I have hers."

"I see," she said.

"And what's that supposed to mean?" he asked.

"I don't know, what does it mean?"

"Nothing." He suddenly looked extremely uncomfortable. He shook his head and focused up at the ceiling. "Nothing."

Nothing? He never said that word that way before. Not even when he told me how the universe would end one day. He said, even then, there would be something left.

Teresa touched his arm. She wanted to touch his face, but he looked so distant; she didn't know if she could reach that far. He wasn't looking at her, that was it. He wasn't thinking of her. She sensed the shift in his attention more than she saw it. The light had been on and now the light was off. *Nothing, nothing at all.* How swift God's universe moved. One moment there was order, the next chaos. The floor could have opened beneath her; already she felt herself falling into a cold abyss. She didn't need to ask the questions but she did anyway.

"Does this *nothing* have a name?" she asked.

He swallowed and nodded. "Yes."

She was having trouble breathing. "Do I know her name?"

122

"Yes."

She choked. "Oh God."

Bill rolled over and took hold of her shoulders. There was pain on his face, but he was no mirror for her because her pain was beyond comprehension. When he spoke, his words sounded so stupid he should have kept his mouth shut.

"I didn't want to hurt you," he said.

"You can't want her instead of me," she whispered.

"Teresa, I didn't *want* any of this."

"Does she know?"

He raised his voice. "Of course she knows! She feels the same way I do. I'm telling you, we didn't want this to happen."

Teresa felt herself going into shock. Her mind couldn't keep up with how fast her heart was sinking. "What happened?" she cried. "What have you two been doing together?"

"Nothing. I swear to you, nothing's happened yet."

She felt so exposed, so used. "Yet?" she croaked. "Is something going to happen?"

"Teresa."

"No! You can't do this to me. I was going to sleep with you next weekend. I was going to love you. I *do* love you. You're my boyfriend. She's my best friend." Teresa wept pitifully. "You're the only friends I have."

Someone knocked at the door.

Bill got up and answered it.

Rene was there. Beautiful Rene.

"Alf decided to walk home," she said quickly to Bill. "And I've discovered that I have a flat tire. I was wondering if I could borrow you to help me . . ." Her gaze strayed inside the apartment. "Teresa?"

"I told her," Bill said quietly.

Rene was sad. They were all so sad. "Oh," Rene said. "Teresa?"

"No." Teresa sat up and wiped her face. "I don't want either of you to say anything. I want to be by myself." She raised her hand when they started to protest. Her fingers shook. "Please do this for me."

"I don't want to leave you alone now," Bill said.

Teresa sighed. "I've been alone before. It's not so bad." She shut her eyes; a red glow burned deep inside her brain. A fire trying to warm a place that was always cold. The place between the living and the dead. She no longer felt totally alive. She only wished somehow that she could die. "Please leave," she whispered.

They did as she asked. They said goodbye and closed the door. She collapsed on the floor and lay there for a very long time.

"They deserve to die," Freedom Jack said when she was finished. "Are you sure you didn't kill them? Is that the reason you're running away from home?"

"I didn't kill them and I'm not running away from home," Teresa said softly. Relating the events had shaken her up some. Her eyes were damp and she raised a hand to swipe at her face. Free reached over and touched her arm.

"I'm sorry," he said quickly. "I didn't mean to be crude. I just hate it when people hurt each other. I always feel like getting back at whoever hurt me. You must have felt the same way."

Teresa forced a smile. "I still do."

"There's always time." Free glanced over his shoulder. "What did you think of her story, Poppy?"

"I think there's more to it," Poppy said.

"They got together—what more is there to say?" Teresa said.

"When did this happen?" Free asked.

"Earlier tonight," Teresa said.

"Well, no wonder you want to get out of town for a few days," Free said. "Did you see either of them just before you left?"

Teresa hesitated. "No."

"There was no point in it, was there?" Free asked, nodding sympathetically. "The past is past is what I say. Let it go, it's dead. Don't you agree, Poppy?"

"Truer words were never spoken," Poppy replied.

Free got angry. "You don't care at all what Teresa's just been through, do you? You think Bill and Rene did the right thing. I know the way your mind works. Come on, say it, whose side are you on?"

"I don't need to answer these questions," Poppy said. "You'll make a liar out of me no matter what I say. But I do care what's happened to Teresa. I think she's been through a difficult time, and I know she's still going through it."

Teresa shook her head. "No, I'm finished with it. Free's right, the past is the past. It's dead."

"We can learn from the past, though," Poppy said.

"Yeah," Free broke in. "We can learn not to trust jerks like Bill and Rene. Ain't that a fact, Teresa?"

"Yeah," Teresa said grimly.

"Bill and Rene are still the same people they were a month ago," Poppy said. "They're still your friends, Teresa."

"I knew it!" Free shouted. "They cheat on Teresa and you think it's all right. You're warped, Poppy. Do you know what those two are probably doing right now? They're probably in bed—you have to forgive me, Teresa, I'm trying to make a point—screwing their brains out. In fact, I bet they had sex with each other right after they met. What do you say, Teresa?"

"I wouldn't put it past them," Teresa said. She appreciated his support, she just wished he wouldn't talk about the betrayal in such graphic language. She *didn't* like what Poppy had to say. It was so easy, she thought, to be philosophical and forgiving when you weren't in the middle of a situation. She bet Poppy had never been dumped in her life.

"Leaving someone can be as hard as being left," Poppy said.

"I can't believe you," Free said, shaking his head in amazement.

"I really don't appreciate your comments," Teresa said to Poppy. "You don't know what happened. You weren't there. I would just as soon you kept your mouth shut."

Poppy didn't answer right away. She took time to light up another cigarette. Finally she spoke, coughing when the air inside the car was unbreathable again.

"I'm sorry," Poppy said.

"Can we talk about something else?" Teresa asked, a note of pleading in her voice. "Tell me more about John, Free. What happened to his hand? Did it get better?"

"It never got better," Free said. "How could it? But I'll tell you about him later. Mother is next on the agenda."

"Where does she live exactly?" Teresa asked.

Free pointed to the dark cliffs up ahead. They were now a long way past San Luis Obispo. The road had begun to rise, to twist and turn. Angry black waves pounded the rocks off to their left and below. A wall of stone stood on their right. The rain continued to fall. It was as if it was never going to stop.

"Not far from here," Free said. "We'll be there soon."

CHAPTER 9

THEY DIDN'T REACH THE PLACE UNTIL AN HOUR LATER. During that time Free leaned back against the seat and took a nap, his snoring rocking softly in rhythm with the turns in the narrow road. In the backseat Poppy sat silent and still. Many times Teresa thought she, too, had drifted off to sleep. But then she'd flick her lighter, the orange flame flaring briefly in Teresa's rearview mirror, and exhale a cloud of fresh smoke. Teresa didn't attempt to make conversation with her. She didn't want to wake Free and she was still mad at Poppy for taking Bill's side in what happened. Oh, Poppy would deny that, Teresa was sure, but it was the truth. Poppy was an ingrate, when you got right down to it. She took and never gave anything in return. One day she'd have to wake up and smell the coffee.

Teresa did not feel well physically. Her fever had begun to subside, but now she was getting the shakes. She turned on the heat, but it didn't work that well because she kept having to roll down the window to get rid of Poppy's cigarette smoke. Her stomach was unsettled. She'd had a few handfuls of Poppy's peanuts and wondered if they were to blame. Nausea pulsed through her in gurgling waves. Each time she thought it was about to end, the sickness would move through her again. She had the flu, she must.

On top of everything else her left wrist started to hurt worse than ever. She had passed the dull ache stage—it was into throbbing now. She honestly wondered if she'd broken it without knowing it. Of course, that should have been impossible. She couldn't even use the hand now to help steer. She was relying solely on her right, dangerous on tight turns. Yet she didn't want to ask Free or Poppy to drive.

She passed maybe three cars on the road, no more.

Lightning flashed far out at sea as she navigated a particularly difficult turn. The trees had begun to thicken on both sides of the road. Thunder rumbled through the branches and shook the dark leaves. Beside her, Free stirred, sat up, and yawned.

"Where are we?" he asked.

"Closing on Big Sur," Teresa said. "But we haven't passed any houses. I think your mom's place must be in front of us."

Free nodded. "It is, it's just around this turn."

Teresa frowned; it was hard to imagine any place could be close. "It's a good thing you woke up when you did or we'd have gone right by it."

"Poppy wouldn't have let us go without paying a visit," Free said. "Isn't that right, Poppy?"

Poppy snorted softly. "I'm not going inside."

Free feigned astonishment. "Don't you want to have your future read?"

"She can't see the future," Poppy said. "She can only read the past."

"But I thought you said we learn from the past?" Free asked innocently.

"I don't want to see the old woman," Poppy repeated. "You don't want to see her either, Teresa, if you have any sense."

"Why not?" Teresa asked, although she had a feeling she wasn't really following the conversation. This woman didn't sound like a normal mother. She fingered her left wrist briefly. Would the thing never stop hurting?

"Because she believes everything she sees in a person," Poppy said. "When a lot of it is just garbage better left ignored."

"My, haven't we become the philosophical critic?" Free said. "You don't want to see her because she'll tell you what a loser you are."

"You can always tell a loser by the company she keeps," Poppy quipped.

Without warning Free held up his hand. "Slow, Teresa. The driveway's coming up in a second."

Teresa squinted through the rain-soaked windshield. "Here? There's nothing here."

Free clapped. "There it is! See? The driveway leads down beside the water. Make a left here."

Free was right. Wow. A narrow driveway that led into a stand of swaying trees appeared on the left. Quickly Teresa twisted the steering wheel around and put mild pressure on the brakes. They crossed the yellow center line and the front of the car dipped down sharply. She pressed the brake harder. The headlights swam around a tunnel of trees. They didn't appear to be redwoods, which confused her. The branches arched over the roof of the car, cutting off the wet sky. Teresa rolled down her window as she moved forward gingerly. She could hear waves crashing, the wind howling. Free squirmed in the seat beside her. He was obviously excited to be seeing his mom again.

"Wait till you see her place," he said. "You won't believe it."

Teresa agreed a moment later, when the tunnel of trees suddenly came to an end and the road emerged close to the ocean and foam-covered rocks with a huge stone castle in the foreground. It was almost medieval, a transplant from dark centuries of fanatical beliefs and cruel punishments. There was no moat, but there could have been. Twisted tree trunks hugged the hard walls, bare branches clawing at the stones. Lightning flashed again, and Teresa thought of wicked witches, haunted woods, and flying bat creatures. She wanted above all else, to go home. Yet that wasn't what she really wanted, she told herself, because she *knew* she couldn't go back. Free had been right when he said the past was dead. The future was all she had left. She brought the car to a halt on the bumpy cobblestone driveway.

"This is too much," she gasped. "Walt Disney must have built this place on drugs." Free laughed and opened his car door.

"I told you I know all the great places to stop," he said, climbing out. "Come along, Teresa. Mother's waiting."

Teresa turned off the engine and glanced in the backseat at Poppy. "Is this place safe?" she asked.

Poppy sighed. "Let's just say you won't die inside."

Curiosity and a desire not to offend Free had her. Teresa glanced once more at the building and cleared her throat. "I suppose that'll have to do," she said.

Free had his garment bag with him as he and Teresa stepped up to the front door. It wasn't an ordinary door, of course, but rather a rectangular gateway into mystery. Free pulled a skeleton key from his back pocket.

"Don't you want to knock?" Teresa asked.

"Mother doesn't like people to knock," Free said confidentially, sliding the key into the lock. Metal scraped metal and the door slowly swung open with protesting creaks. Just before they stepped inside, Teresa glanced over her shoulder and saw Poppy leaning her head back on the seat as if, finally, the strange girl was going to take a short rest.

Short?

Teresa had no idea how long they'd be inside. She checked her watch. It was four in the morning. God, the night seemed as if it would never end.

Inside was an entranceway of lit torches and shadows plucked from a horror movie set that had long been abandoned. The air was damp and the stone walls oozed moisture. They crept through a claustrophobic passageway into an immense hall filled with the sound of their own footsteps echoing over and over. The light from the torches was swallowed up by the rich darkness. Teresa put her hand, her sore left hand, on Free's arm and whispered the words that had been on the tip of her tongue since they had turned off the main road.

"What are we doing here?" she asked.

"I told you, seeing mother," he replied.

"Does your mother really live in this tomb?"

"You don't like the decor?"

"It scares me."

Free nodded. "I think that's the point of it. Anyway, I call her mother. We're very close, you understand. But my real mother died a long time ago."

"How did you come to know this person?" she asked.

"She read my fortune." Free gripped her left arm, steering her the way he wanted her to go. He gestured to the right, but to the right of what she wasn't sure. The place was a walk through the history of the earth. "She likes to sit in a small room over here when she gives readings."

"Does she know we're coming?" Teresa asked.

"Yes."

"How?"

"She's a fortune teller. She tells her own fortune every morning when she gets up and knows who's coming to visit." Free grinned. "It beats having to keep an appointment book."

They found the woman sitting in what appeared to be a library. The walls were lined with books, dark and dusty volumes of all sizes with barely legible fading titles. Between the sections of shelves hung maps of places Teresa did not recognize, continents that weren't on the globe. Huge candles flickered in the four corners of the room. The woman looked up as they entered and smiled with thin red lips.

Her hair was snow white, long like her heavy purple dress. The fine wisps of aged thread almost disappeared into the darkness that hugged her sides. Her eyes were striking, blue and hard, like bits of coral that had been removed from an ocean depth where the sun never shined. She was old, extremely, Teresa thought, her skin lined with time that had not passed easily. But she was not feeble. She crooked a beckoning finger to them as she smiled and gestured for them to sit in front of her on two small wooden stools. They did so.

"Welcome," she said in a dry voice that sounded as if it had little, if any, breath supporting it. The old woman sat on an overstuffed chair beside a low round wooden table littered with a star atlas, scraps of wrinkled paper, two inkwell pens, and a silver pyramid the size of a grapefruit. Teresa forced a smile, although she felt like getting up and running out the door as fast as possible. This person, she was sure, this *hag,* was not going to tell her anything she wanted to hear.

"Hello," Teresa said.

"Hi, mother," Free said casually, setting his garment bag on the stone floor and crossing his legs.

"Your name, child?" the woman asked.

Teresa hesitated. "Teresa."

"Your full name," the woman insisted.

"Teresa Marie Chafey."

"What time were you born? What day?"

"I was born at exactly ten in the morning on a Saturday," Teresa said. "My birthday's November twelfth. I'm now eighteen years old so I was born in—"

"I do not need the year," the woman interrupted. She turned to her star atlas. "The year is always the same. It doesn't change with the sun or the moon."

"Huh?" Teresa said.

134

"Mother doesn't do the usual astrological chart," Free whispered in her ear.

They waited silently while the woman performed her calculations. Soon she had a sheet of orange paper in her hand sprinkled with numbers, astrological signs, and a few strange symbols Teresa had never seen before. An amusing thought—it was amusing given the circumstances—floated through her head.

I wonder how much this woman charges.

"You've had a difficult life," the old woman began after consulting her paper one last time. "Your parents don't care for you and you don't care for them. You have been alone most of your life, even when surrounded by other people. You think you are different from everyone else and you're right. You do not belong in crowds because the crowd does not appreciate your uniqueness. Your talent is vast. You can write poetry and prose, play instruments, and sing like a goddess. All three of these abilities appear to you to be separate, but they are one and the same. You can touch people, that's your gift. Yet you do not like to be touched yourself. You have built walls to keep the world out and the world, in turn, has built walls to keep you inside. That is how you suffer. Any time you step outside your usual place, and demonstrate what you have to offer, people reward you by throwing stones. Am I not correct, Teresa Chafey?"

"Yes," Teresa whispered. She was shivering before she entered the castle, now she froze. The old woman's voice was cold, and it penetrated deep. The truth could do that.

How does she know all this about me? I've never met her until tonight.

A mystery. The building was a mystery. The woman was an enigma. Her hard blue eyes burned with the flame from a candle. She was waiting for Teresa to ask a question. Another mystery, that the old hag would have no trouble unraveling. That's what scared Teresa most, that she was sitting before a crystal ball that glittered as no mirror could. The woman was just that—a mirror reflecting the person who was sitting in front of her.

Teresa didn't want to go forward, not yet. She wanted to better understand why her past had died the death it had.

"Why did my boyfriend want Rene instead of me?" she asked.

"Because you scared him," the woman said. "He didn't know what you'd do next."

Teresa chuckled uneasily. "Bill wasn't afraid of me."

"Not of you, but of what you would do. They are not the same thing, child. Often, they have nothing in common."

"Was there another reason?" Teresa asked.

"The reason I have given you is enough. But if you must have another one, I'd say Rene and Bill wanted to be close to each other in a way neither wanted to be close to you. Because"—the woman paused to scratch her chin with a long golden nail—"they couldn't understand you. People always fear what they cannot understand."

"You come back to fear," Teresa said.

"You come back to it. I merely speak what I see. What do you fear, child?"

Teresa suddenly felt defiant. It was not pleasant,

having her brain picked, even when she'd asked for it. But was that true? She hadn't exactly asked to have her fortune read. Free had just dragged her into this place.

"You tell me," Teresa said.

"You are afraid to be alone." She consulted her paper again. "But you can have love in your life if you don't care how much it costs. You can have it tonight, now, in this place. But you do not want love. You want adoration, and that's cheap. How much do you want to spend tonight, Teresa?"

Teresa stammered. "I don't understand what you're asking."

The woman leaned closer. Her dark blue eyes, though, did not move in sync with the rest of her. They seemed, for a moment, stuck in the space they had occupied since they had entered the room. The eyes could have slipped back into the old woman's forehead; they appeared to peer at Teresa from beneath the weathered flesh, from a perspective that had nothing to do with modern-day humanity. Teresa had mentally compared the woman to a witch when she first saw her. Now she believed the comparison valid. The woman terrified her.

The hag twisted her thin red lips once more into that grotesque thin line that was supposed to pass as a smile.

"How come you haven't asked me why Bill didn't want to sleep with you?" the old woman asked.

Teresa swallowed and lied. "I did sleep with him." She glanced over at Free and added, "A few times."

The old woman moved in close. "You drove Bill away."

Teresa barely shook her head. She could smell the woman's breath; the taste of copper in it. The hag could have had a mouth full of blood. "Bill didn't leave me because he was afraid of having sex with me," Teresa said.

The old woman raised a balding eyebrow. "Then how did you know I was suggesting that?"

"I just knew."

"When you have sex with someone you become wedded to that person, and Bill was afraid to be wedded to you, Teresa. He was afraid of where you were going."

"You just said he was afraid of what I might do."

The woman nodded and sat back. "What you have done has determined where you're going." She paused. "Do you want me to speak of your future?"

"No," Teresa said.

"You are soon to have the things you craved from Bill. The things he didn't want to give you."

"I told you not to tell me."

The old woman cackled. The sound was like the screech of nails on a chalkboard. "Why shouldn't I tell you? It doesn't cost you or me a cent. My advice is as cheap as the things you are about to receive."

Teresa stood. "Thank you for your time. I'm leaving." She turned and strode out of the room, into the vast cavern where both light and direction were confused. Free caught up with her before she could run into a wall.

"Hold on," he said, grabbing her by the arm. "Don't be angry."

She turned on him. "Why did you take me to this awful place?"

138

"I thought you'd have fun."

"I'm not having fun."

"Well, then, I was wrong," Free said. "But that's still no reason to leave in such a hurry. Let me show you the rest of the place first. There are rooms in here that'll take your breath away."

"No. I hate this place. I just want to get out of here."

"You have to see one room, at least. It's where I sleep when I stay here."

Teresa shivered in the oppressive gloom. "I can't believe you actually stay here with that old witch. She doesn't even look like a human being."

Free was amused. "She isn't human. She's just an apparition. You can close your eyes and blow hard and she'll vanish." He touched the tip of her nose with his finger. "Close your eyes, Teresa. Let me lead you to a special place."

He was speaking to her in his story-telling voice. The voice he used to make the pictures shine with words that told her of John and Candy. Their whole lives had been laid out in the space of a few hours together in the car. He had magic words, just like his magic fingers. She remembered then that she had forgotten to check to see if there was a joker in her back pocket, after all.

Free slowly pulled her forward while she kept her eyes squeezed shut. She trusted him, it was true, but it was equally true that she was afraid to open her eyes and see where she was going. Or to open them and reach in her pocket to discover that Freedom Jack had been wrong about the joker. That it might not be a joke at all, the whole thing, what they were doing tonight.

Time passed as if in a dream. Could a person fall asleep on her feet? Perhaps Teresa did, even with her feet moving. Free's voice seemed to come to her from far away.

"Open your eyes, Teresa," Free said. "We must have a toast."

She opened her eyes. He was standing in front of her with a bottle of red wine and two glasses in his hands. Torches on the wall beside him burned angrily. Teresa saw that she was upstairs now—that she must have climbed steps in her brief trance—and that she was standing in a huge bedroom with open windows that looked out over the turbulent sea. The salty wind tugged at her hair. Free took a step toward her and handed her a glass. He uncorked the bottle in a blur, using his magician speed.

"This wine is very old," he said and poured the dark liquid into her glass. "Very fine."

"I shouldn't drink, I'm driving," she said.

"Nonsense," he said, pouring himself a glass, too. He startled her by suddenly tossing what was left of the wine over his shoulder into the fireplace not far from the opulent bed. The glass shattered and then— to her amazement—the fireplace ignited. Flames leaped up the chimney and the room began to warm, despite the breeze pouring in through the windows from the ocean. Free took another step toward her, until he was practically standing on top of her. He raised his glass and clinked their crystal. "To Teresa Marie Chafey," he said. "May her shivers pass swiftly." He sipped the wine.

"How do you know I'm shaking?" she asked.

"I know your wrist hurts. I know you feel sick to

your stomach. I know because I know everything." He leaned over and kissed her on the forehead. His breath was cool but his lips were warm and she felt his touch as if he had, in one move, caressed her entire body. "Drink your wine, Teresa," he whispered in her ear. "It will help you through this bad time."

Teresa tasted the wine. It was warm, thick, like fresh orange juice with plenty of pulp. Had it not tasted so good, though, she would have thought she was drinking human blood. It looked like it. In an instant her nausea began to recede. She took a larger drink and the throbbing in her wrist lessened.

"It's good," she mumbled.

"You're good." He kissed her ear, her hair, moving slowly back to her face. He kissed her eyebrows and dropped his glass on the floor and the glass splattered at their feet. Fortunately, the wine did not ignite as that in the bottle had. Or maybe it did; she suddenly felt as if she were standing in a pool of flames. The moment was pure eroticism, pleasurable beyond belief. Free tilted her face up and began to kiss her mouth, deep kisses, that made her feel as if she were naked.

You're so bad.

He could read her mind, that boy. He took the glass out of her hand and led her to the bed where she stretched out beside him and threw her arms around his neck, while his hands moved over her body to places Bill had never wanted to venture. But Teresa did not think about her boyfriend then, nor did she think of Poppy, waiting outside in the car. Her passion consumed her, and maybe the old hag was right and it was cheap, but Teresa felt it was high time she had got a bargain. Free's mouth was all over her, and the wine in his mouth darkened her skin in places where he caressed her so that, yes, once more, it looked as if the beverage was blood, making her believe that she was bleeding and being eaten by the boy who was making love to her. Yet she laughed at the thought, in her ecstasy. It was all a dream, it must be. Right then, she couldn't even remember having left home.

The growing sensations in her body took her mind and blew it out the open windows on the cold wind. Out over the sea, which foamed like a cauldron full of witch's brew. There she saw tall towers in the distance, fortresses of stone and steel built by old wizards and dark lords to defend realms founded on black magic and sharp sword. Her mind flew like a wraith through the dead past, while her body shuddered in the eternal present. The moment was rich. She told herself, in the vacuum that had once contained her thoughts, that it didn't matter if she could remember everything she had done that night. She was enjoying herself.

CHAPTER 10

THEY DROVE NORTH THROUGH THE STORM. TERESA didn't know what time it was. She had left her watch at the old hag's place, along with her virginity, wrapped in sheets wrinkled with fading pleasure. Her bodily aches had returned; they had been there the moment Free shook her awake and told her to get dressed because they had to hurry. Along with all her earlier complaints, her head now hurt. She longed for a couple of aspirins. She didn't know what the hurry was, but Free said they had to get somewhere before the sun came up. She hoped Poppy wasn't still planning on seeing her father, the priest.

Free sat silently beside her, staring straight ahead at the road. It was Poppy's turn to speak and she was narrating the remainder of Candy's tale.

"As I said, Candy had a newborn baby, no money, no skills, and no man," Poppy said. "But she loved her little Johnny, and Candy blossomed when she was in love. She stayed in Oregon, but moved to Portland so that she could try to go back to school. At first that was impossible—Johnny needed too much attention —and she had to remain on welfare and stay at home, which was a postage stamp-size apartment. She drew a lot during these days, mainly sketches of her son. She couldn't afford a camera or film to take pictures of him. She refused to ask anybody for help: Henry, her parents—she didn't want charity from anybody. She despised being on welfare and got off it as soon as she could. It was a big deal for Candy to be self-sufficient. She felt it had been her dependence on John in high school that had led to so much misery in both their lives. Where John was, what he was doing—she had no idea. She had tried, again, in vain to find him. Yet she knew in her heart that he was not doing well. It was almost as if, when she held her son, she could feel John's pain.

"Candy had discarded the idea of becoming a doctor, and with a kid to raise she didn't want to risk trying to make it as an artist. When Johnny was a year and a half, old enough to be left with a sitter, she took a job as a waitress at a nearby restaurant and began to attend night classes at the University of Oregon. The classes she had taken at Berkeley were transferrable and she set to work trying to get into a nursing program at the university. It was a long way from being a doctor but that didn't bother Candy because as a nurse she would still get to help people. Also, from research she knew that nurses could have control over when they worked. They could do three twelve-hour shifts and take the rest of the week off. Candy thought that would be perfect. She could support herself and her son and still be around to watch him grow up.

"Candy was able to enter the nursing program after only one more year of regular courses. The studying was hard for her, particularly when she was tired from working and taking care of her son. With her job, she made little more than she did on welfare, but Candy began to feel pride in herself and her abilities.

"The program lasted two years and she made it through. She didn't graduate at the top of her class. In fact, she almost failed a couple of courses. But when she went searching for a job, the hospitals scarcely glanced at her grades. She was an R.N. and they were in short supply. She got a job almost immediately, and for the first time in a long time she had money for herself and her son, who was now almost ready to enter kindergarten.

"The first thing Candy bought was a new car. She had spent the previous three years riding around town on a bike. She was in good shape, but she was tired of not being able to sit in comfort and listen to the stereo while she went from place to place. The car was nothing extravagant—a stripped-down import—but she loved it. So did Johnny. He liked to sit up front and point out and name everything in town. He had an extraordinary vocabulary for a kid. He was smart as a whip—Candy thought he would be the one to become a doctor. In fact, she began to call him Doc, which made him laugh.

"On a rare trip down to L.A. to visit her parents, Candy met a guy. He wasn't a doctor. He worked nights as a custodian at a local high school. That may not sound glamorous, but *he* was. His name was Clyde and he was almost as wild as John had been. Candy liked him right away and he fell head over heels for her. They met at a park near her parents' house. She had brought Johnny there to fly a kite. Clyde was chasing the ducks down by the pond. He said his niece wanted one for her birthday, and by golly, she was going to have one. They never did catch a duck, and Johnny let go of his kite and the wind took it away. Clyde got her number, though, and called her the same night. They went to dinner and a movie, the same thing the next night. Candy wasn't in L.A. long. She was back home in Oregon only a few days when Clyde showed up at her doorstep. He said he happened to be in the neighborhood.

"Clyde pursued Candy inexhaustibly. Every weekend he drove up from L.A. to Portland to see her. He was serious. He asked her to marry him when they had been going together three months. Candy laughed the first time he asked—she thought he was joking. But then he brought her a diamond ring the next day. She was afraid to try it on. She liked Clyde, she may even have loved him, but it was all happening too fast for her. She told him she needed more time. One thing, though, that might surprise you. Clyde was able to talk Candy into moving back down to L.A. Recently, Candy and her parents had grown closer. They loved Johnny, and Candy decided it was unfair to deprive them of the company of their only grandchild. Also, Oregon was beautiful but it wasn't home. Candy was an L.A. girl, even with the city's smog and traffic and other problems.

"She moved back and got her own apartment, even though Clyde objected. He wanted her to live with him. She couldn't, yet she was moving closer to accepting his marriage proposal. Clyde didn't plan on remaining a janitor forever. Now that he no longer had to drive up to see her, he switched to working days so he could go to school at night. He wanted to be a school teacher. He loved working with kids. He got along great with Johnny. Candy would watch the two of them playing together and wonder what was making her hesitate. She didn't wonder too long to realize what it was. She didn't love Clyde the same way she had loved John. It was the same old thing she had experienced with Henry.

"But Candy wasn't thinking about John the night she ran out late at night to buy a carton of cigarettes. Clyde was staying overnight at her place. She got off work about nine and had spent the evening watching rented movies with Clyde. It was maybe one in the morning. Johnny was long asleep. Clyde didn't go to the store with her because he had to stay to watch Johnny and because he didn't approve of her habit. He used to say to her, "You're a nurse. You know what those things do to your lungs and heart." But Candy had been smoking since high school, and even John had been unable to get her to quit.

"Candy had been back in L.A. about three months at this time. She had an excellent job at a hospital about two miles from her apartment. It was a rainy night and she was tired but feeling content. In fact, as she drove to the all-night mini-mart near her place she thought that her life had finally begun to turn around. She had financial stability and a man who loved her. Her son was healthy. On the drive to get her cigarettes Candy counted her blessings. But blessings are not like gold coins. You can't count them and lock them in a safe and expect to find them there later. Candy had been tossed around by fate all her life, and fate's kind of like a kid who has found a nice ball to play with, a ball that bounces back. The kid will keep playing with the ball until it goes flat or she loses it. Candy was about to lose something that night, though she didn't know it.

"She parked in front of the mini-mart. She had been there a dozen times late at night, usually to get cigarettes and maybe fill up her gas tank. The place was always open. She got out of her car and walked toward the door. She walked fast—the rain was coming down hard and she didn't want to get wet. It was only when she had her hand on the door, and was about to open it, that she raised her eyes and saw the man inside with the gun in his hand, pointed at the head of the store owner. Her breath stuck in her chest. She knew she should turn and run away, call the police. But she blinked and peered closer. The man looked familiar. It was John, her long-lost love. John was robbing this store. That was terrible, she thought, there must be some mistake. She opened the door and stepped inside."

"Stop right there," Free interrupted.

"Why?" Poppy asked.

"Yeah, why?" Teresa asked. She wanted to hear the end of the story; she had waited so long to hear it. The tale helped distract her from her nausea and her burning wrist. The skin below her left hand could have had a torch on it, it hurt so much. She was going to have to take something for the pain soon.

"I want to tell this part," Free said. "You'll screw it up, Poppy. You'll change things around and give Teresa the wrong idea."

"Very well," Poppy said. "Give us John's version of the night of the holdup."

"In a few minutes," Free said. "First I want to explain how John happened to be there that night. Listen closely, Poppy, you might learn a thing or two."

"I doubt it," Poppy muttered.

CHAPTER 11

"JOHN WAS NOW A HEROIN ADDICT. LIKE I SAID BEFORE, he supported his habit by robbing soda and candy machines and phone booths. His addiction defined him. The drug was the center of his life, and he spent most of his time trying to figure out how to continue to supply himself. To make more out of what he did get ahold of, he began to mainline. He injected the boiled drug directly into his veins. It made the high more powerful, yet, at the same time, he needed more of the drug to attain the same high. Like every other junkie, he took one step forward and two back.

"The pain in his hand only left him when he was high, and he could not stay high twenty-four hours a day so he went through a lot of bad times. The surgeons had done a poor job grafting the skin around his wound. He was prone to infections in his right hand, and was constantly having to buy antibiotics as well as heroin. His habit was now costing him five hundred bucks a day. Do you know how many quarters that is? Two thousand. That's a lot of machines to rob just to stay even. It was hopeless, really, he had to go on to bigger game.

"John started to break into houses in middle-class neighborhoods. He got to be something of an expert when it came to casing out houses. He never broke into homes when he thought people were there. Of course he miscalculated a few times and nearly got his brains blown out. But he wouldn't carry a gun. He didn't want to hurt anybody, and never really had except for the time he punched Sims in the mouth.

"His hand worked against him as a thief. Too many tasks that went with the territory, like picking locks and silently lifting stuck windows, required two good hands. When he did get inside, he was able only to steal small stuff: jewelry, watches, cash. Occasionally he'd swipe a portable stereo or a VCR. But he had to resell the stuff for pennies because he could only do business with the blackest part of the black market. His main drug supplier, an addict himself, suggested he do a little dealing on the side to help make ends meet. Being a pusher wasn't John's style—besides, it was dangerous. He only tried it for a couple weeks when he was robbed in the middle of the night by a guy with a switchblade. John lost his entire supply of drugs and two pints of blood. The assailant laid John's belly wide open. He had to rush to the hospital holding his guts in. It took forty stitches to sew him back together. John was pretty hardened to the horrors of life by this time, but that incident scared him badly. He went back to straight stealing, a safe occupation. Man, life sucked, it really did.

"John was back in the hospital not long after that. He had caught another type of infection—hepatitis. A dirty needle was no doubt to blame. He didn't want to go into the hospital, but the doctor he saw told him he'd die if he didn't and the way John felt he figured the man was probably right. He had never been so sick in his life. He couldn't walk across the room without having to stop and rest.

"He had a problem with the hospital, though, once he was inside. They wouldn't give him any heroin, of course. But then, they wouldn't even give him methadone to help him with withdrawal. His doctor explained that he had to be in a special program to get methadone, and that it was an out-patient program only. You couldn't be *in* the hospital and join. John took the news hard. He was sick from hepatitis and from withdrawal. To top it off his old friend Mr. Three-Fingered Hand was complaining. He couldn't take the pain, he just couldn't. And it wasn't his fault. Pain can make a proud man humble. Pain can make a good man turn bad.

"One evening when John had been in the hospital a couple of days, he got out of bed around nine o'clock, wearing only a bathrobe, and went searching for a nurses' station that had been left unattended. He didn't wait till later because he knew the nurses changed shifts at nine, and he hoped to take advantage of the change in shifts. The hospital was full of places to snitch drugs. John didn't want much, just a little something to knock him out so he could sleep. That wasn't much to ask, but the nurses in his ward wouldn't give him anything stronger than Tylenol. What was Tylenol to a heroin addict? It was like giving cookies to a hungry tiger.

"John didn't find any drugs. He had only searched a couple of floors when he spotted a nurse at the far end of the hall. She had her back to him and was waiting for the elevator. She appeared to be going off duty. Even from behind she looked familiar to John. He moved a few steps closer, hanging on to a laundry basket to keep from falling over. He really shouldn't have been out of bed. The elevator door opened and a guy about twenty-five years old accompanied by a kid who was maybe five stepped into the hall. The nurse shouted with pleasure. The two had obviously surprised her by coming to pick her up at work. The little boy ran into the nurse's arms shouting Mommy, and the guy hugged the woman and the two of them had a long kiss.

"John saw the nurse's face when she let go of the guy. He recognized her in an instant. It was Candy. He almost died right then. I mean, he was close to dying and in the space of two seconds he took a huge step closer. His heart just broke. Candy, his girl, in the arms of some jerk. And with a kid—John couldn't stop staring at the boy. He looked like his child, he really did. Certainly, he didn't look like he belonged to the gorilla hugging Candy. The feeling that his family had been stolen from him, without his knowing it, overwhelmed John. He sagged against the wall. It was a miracle he didn't collapse on the floor.

"Then Candy turned and stared straight at him—but she didn't see him. Oh, she saw a patient, a very sick young man. But she didn't see John. He could have been invisible, as invisible as he had been the last few years. Nevertheless, she raised a hand to her face and took a step in his direction. She was maybe a hundred feet away.

"'Do you need help, sir?' she asked.

"A tear ran down John's face. He shook his head.

"'Get back to bed,' Candy called. 'You'll feel better soon.'

"John nodded. Candy turned and disappeared into the elevator with her family. He thought they looked happy together.

"John walked back to his room and changed into the clothes he had been wearing when he entered the hospital. He left without checking out. The night sky was filled with clouds. His car was parked in the lot, an old piece of junk that wasn't worth the cost of the registration sticker on the license plate. It was all he had left in the world. He didn't even have his memories anymore. Because the only ones he had cherished had been from his time in high school with Candy. But now she had stolen them from him, turned them to grief. He blamed her for not waiting for him. It sounds crazy, but in his heart he had always believed he'd find her again and that they would be together. Just as soon as he got his life back on track, he had told himself. But now there was no possibility of that. His life was over—he felt it end when he saw her beautiful face at the end of the hall. Yeah, she was still as beautiful, after all these years, and here he was a corpse just waiting to start rotting.

"John needed a fix in the worst way. He drove to his most trusted friend, his pusher. The bastard wouldn't give him any heroin. He wanted money, and John didn't have any. John pleaded with him, but it was like pleading with the devil to please lower the thermostat. Yet the guy did do something John wouldn't have expected. He ran in the back and got an unmarked handgun and gave it to him. John just stared at the gun. He had never used one before and tonight was not a good night to start. His left hand was shaking along with his right because he was so weak.

" 'Pull a job, bring me some cash,' his friend said. 'Then I'll see what I can do for you.'

"John nodded. He left the place. He still didn't want to hurt anybody, but everybody was hurting him. All he wanted was one fix, just one shot straight into his veins and he knew he'd be able to think clearly again. He imagined that if he could just get that one fix he might check himself back into the hospital. Then maybe Candy would drop down a couple of floors and nurse him back to health. He laughed at the absurdity of the idea as he drove through the stormy night, the rain plastering his windshield, his tears plastering his face. He knew he wasn't going back to the hospital. He knew he was going nowhere.

"He drove for a long time before he spotted a store that looked deserted enough to hit. But he hadn't gone far because he drove mainly in circles. He parked in front of the mini-mart and climbed out into the night. He was wet, he was cold. He staggered toward the door. He couldn't see anyone inside except for the short fellow behind the counter. He figured he'd whip out his gun, get the money, and be gone in the blink of an eye. He was thinking about how good the fix would feel bubbling in his veins when he opened the door and stepped inside. He had the gun hidden in his belt under his coat. He was so out of it he hadn't even checked to see if it was loaded.

"He didn't stride straight up to the counter and get down to the robbing business, however. He wasn't sure why, but it might have been because he was inexperienced. After he was inside the store, he thought it might be a good idea to first browse around, maybe pick out a few items, and then saunter up to the counter. Then, when the guy was ringing up the stuff he could whip out his gun. Yeah, he thought, that sounded like a plan. Even a dying man needed a plan. The guy in the store followed his every move.

"John picked out items that he actually wanted: a six-pack of beer, a box of doughnuts, a carton of milk. He didn't know if he would be able to keep any of the food down, he'd been vomiting nonstop for the last week, but he thought the stuff would be better than what they'd been trying to feed him at the hospital. He walked up to the counter and piled the goods up. The employee looked him over real close and asked to see his I.D. That made John laugh.

"'I look like I'm ready to bury and you want to see if I'm legal?' John asked. 'Sure, I'll show you my I.D. I've got it right here.'

"John pulled out his gun and pointed it at the guy, who immediately raised his hands. Yet he didn't look that surprised. It was as if he got held up regularly. John told him to give him every dollar he had. The guy popped the cash register and began to stack the dollar bills on the counter. John thought he was doing pretty well for a first timer.

"Then a young woman entered the store. John

glanced over at her and almost dropped his gun. It was Candy, but it couldn't be Candy, he thought. Not twice in the same day. Man, talk about fate. It was a night of nightmares. Candy had her eyes open now. She ran toward him, calling his name.

"At the same time the guy behind the counter crouched down, going almost out of sight, reaching for something that John would have bet the clothes he was standing in was a gun. John didn't want the guy to come back up shooting. So he fired a shot into the bottles on the wall behind the counter. Seagram 7 splattered everywhere and the air was thick with the smell of whiskey.

"'I wouldn't if I was you,' John told the guy. Slowly the man began to stand back up, his hands in the air once more. All this time, of course, John had Candy hurrying toward him calling his name. Well, she had never had good timing, he thought. He shook his gun in her direction and shouted, 'Stay!'

"Candy stopped. She stared at him with her big brown eyes. 'It's me, John,' she said.

"'I don't know any John,' he said.

"She took a step toward him. She didn't even have the decency to put her hands in the air and here it was his first holdup. 'That's not going to work,' she said. 'I know who you are and you know who I am.' She grimaced. 'What are you doing with that gun? You look terrible.'

"He sneered. 'I'm sorry I didn't have a chance to get the gun color coordinated with my outfit. Get the hell out of here, Candy. Can't you see I'm busy?'

"She was ashen, an improvement, though, over John's color. His hepatitis had turned him the color of a sick lemon. She took another step toward him. Not many more and she would be able to reach out and take the gun from him.

" 'It was you I saw at the hospital this evening,' she said.

" 'It took you long enough to notice,' he said.

" 'That means you're sick,' she said. 'You should be in bed.' She stopped and grimaced again. 'What happened to your hand?'

"That question really annoyed John. He hadn't seen her in God knows how long and she had to immediately point out his most sensitive flaw. I tell you, that Candy had no class.

" 'I got it caught in a hot dog bun machine,' he said bitterly, his voice cracking. 'But I don't want to talk about it right now. I want you to get out of here. I want you to go home to your husband and your son and I want you to leave me alone!' John fired another shot into the whiskey bottles, the dark liquid and the glass flying everywhere. The guy behind the counter had begun to fidget in ways John didn't appreciate. 'You finish counting out my money or I'll kill you!' he screamed.

"The guy got back to work emptying the cash register. Candy just stood where she was, staring at John. He was surprised when she started weeping. 'What's happened to you?' she cried. 'Why are you doing this?'

"He never did get a chance to tell her why because right then all three of them heard police sirens. They were close. It sounded as if the cops would be there in seconds. That they were heading straight for the store

John didn't doubt for a second. He realized the guy behind the counter must have pressed a button the instant John pulled the gun. No wonder the guy had been emptying the register so slowly. He knew he had help coming.

" 'Dammit!' John swore. He switched the gun to his bad hand and tried scooping the money off the counter with his left and into his pockets. But he was in too much of a hurry and most of it ended up on the floor. The sirens grew louder. They were practically outside the door! He wouldn't be able to go out the front way, he realized. He'd have to try to escape out the back. He turned away from Candy. He could see the rear exit at the end of a narrow dark hallway.

" 'Don't run, John!' Candy cried at his back. 'They'll kill you!'

"He was in no mood to listen to her. He might have been if he hadn't seen her that evening at the hospital with her family. He might have become a changed man right then, just knowing she was around. But she had let him down again. She had cheated on him with another man. He ran down the hallway toward the rear exit.

"It was locked. His luck was rotten. He pounded on the wire mesh door with his bad hand and his pain and sorrow and fear in that moment were of truly tragic proportions. He was a trapped and wounded animal. He glanced back the way he had come. The other guy had guts, John had to hand it to him. Even with the police only seconds away, he was going for his gun. John pointed his own in the guy's direction, just above his head, and let loose a shot. The bullet hit the front window of the store and the entire sheet of glass collapsed. The checker jumped and raised his hands over his head.

"John ran back to the front of the store. He was passing the counter when two police officers pounced inside, their revolvers drawn.

"'Freeze!' they shouted in unison.

"John froze for only a second. Then he did something he wouldn't have believed he'd have done in a million years. Of course, that was just the point. He had only a split second to react. He grabbed Candy and placed her in front of him as a shield. She didn't make a sound. Hanging on to her by the hair, he raised his gun to her head.

"'Drop your guns!' John ordered. 'If you don't, I'll kill her.'

"The police glanced at each other. They were young, inexperienced. They had made a mistake—both coming into the store at the same time. John could see only one car outside. They had no backup. They were scared. They didn't want to drop their guns. They had no idea what he would do. He had no idea. He just wanted a moment to think, to have a shot of heroin and be at peace. Or maybe just a moment to talk to Candy. He had a gun to her head, true, but right then he imagined a talk might be nice; that she might be able to set his mind and body at peace.

"'John,' Candy said calmly. 'I have to tell you something.'

"Her speaking surprised him. She should have been crying or screaming, but she said his name so normally he couldn't help but respond. 'What?' he asked.

"She didn't get a chance to answer him. One of the

cops had dropped his gun, but the other wasn't going to chance it. He wasn't going to risk his life, although he was all too happy to risk the life of an innocent bystander. He aimed his gun at John, who stood ever so slightly to the left of Candy. Naturally, though, being half a foot taller than Candy, John was exposed. The cop fired.

"The bullet caught John in the side of the neck. It hit him with the force of a freight train. John let go of Candy and dropped to his knees. His blood gushed over his shirt. The cop fired again. This bullet caught John in the belly. It tore open the scar where he had been knifed. More blood poured out. That was all John could see for a moment, his life draining away from him onto the dirty floor of the mini-mart. He didn't want it to end this way, looking down into the dirt. He spent the last few years of his life crawling in the mud and he wanted to go out with a vision of something beautiful. He looked up and saw Candy staring down at him. She smiled, he thought she smiled. Suddenly everything started to go dark. But he still had his gun in his hand, he could feel it. Oddly enough, he had it in his right hand, and the fingers, in the last few seconds of his life, even the phantom fingers, suddenly stopped hurting. His whole hand felt whole again. It was the most wonderful feeling. He flexed his hand.

"Well, can I say that and have you believe it? Or should I just say he pointed the gun at Candy and fired? That would probably be closer to the truth because he did shoot her. And it would be fair to say he wanted to, either because of what she had done to him or simply because he didn't want to die alone on the dirty floor. He shot Candy in the heart, and her smile faded as a big dark stain formed in the center of her shirt. He watched her fall toward the floor, slowly. But he didn't see her hit. He heard another shot, and it must have been from the cop because his own gun had fallen out of his hand. He saw a flash of red. He heard an eerie *splat* sound. As he fell backward, he figured it must have been the sound of his brains hitting the wall behind him.

"He died, they both did. But doesn't everybody?"

Free paused. "And that's the story of John and Candy."

"God," Teresa whispered, shocked by the sudden violent ending.

"Would you say I described everything accurately, my dear?" Free asked Poppy.

"Just beautifully, Jack," Poppy said.

CHAPTER 12

THEY DIDN'T TALK MUCH AFTER THE DEATH OF JOHN and Candy. Free leaned back and began to snore softly. Poppy did not resume her endless chain-smoking. But periodically she would flick her lighter, stare at the flame for a few seconds, and then put it out. Teresa, for her part, continued to fight against the pain in her body. She searched for a place to turn off and buy aspirin. Several times she thought she'd have to pull over to the side and vomit. In reality, the farther she went, the more confused she became about their whereabouts. They had passed San Luis Obispo enough hours ago that they should have entered Big Sur. And they had entered a wooded area, but the trees were not redwoods. She didn't know what they were except that they were tall and dark and incredibly bunched together. The branches on the trees frightened her. They hung like tired arms, and sometimes they shook even when the wind wasn't blowing. She could no longer see the ocean, although she believed she could hear it. The sound of water had followed her since she got in her car earlier that evening: falling rain and crashing waves—water running, as she was running.

Finally, though, the rain began to let up.

"We're almost there," Poppy said suddenly after a silence that could have lasted an hour.

"Almost where?" Teresa asked.

"My father's place," Poppy said.

Teresa groaned. She really wasn't in the mood for games. "The church?" she asked.

"Yes," Poppy said. "Can we stop there?"

"I really don't think so," Teresa said, annoyed. "I don't feel good and I want to get to San Francisco before I collapse. Would it be all right with you if we skip the social call? Your father must be in bed at this time anyway."

"He's awake," Poppy said.

"Poppy?"

"What?"

"I told you, I don't want to stop. This is my car and I'm driving. You should respect that and not bother me."

Poppy was silent a moment. "You'll feel better if you let my father hear your confession."

"How will going to confession make me feel better? I have a headache. My wrist is aching, I've got the shakes, and I want to throw up. I need a doctor, I don't need a priest."

"I can't force you to stop," Poppy said.

Teresa snorted. "Well, I'm glad to hear that."

"But you have nowhere else to stop."

Teresa paused. "What do you mean?"

"You've been looking for a turnoff for a while now. You haven't seen any. You won't see any until you come to the church. And who can say what comes after that?"

Teresa was incredulous. "That's the most ridiculous thing I've ever heard. There'll be plenty of places to stop just as soon as we get out of these woods. Soon we'll be in Carmel and then Monterey."

"Is the road to those places open?" Poppy asked. "How many cars have you seen coming from the other way?"

"A few, not many."

"You haven't seen any lately," Poppy said. "Stop at the church, rest for a while. Get your strength back, you're going to need it."

"For what?" Teresa asked.

"Who knows?" Poppy said.

Teresa squeezed the steering wheel. Her palms were still clammy; they were practically dripping onto the wheel. It made no sense; she had never felt this way before. It must be all the cigarette smoke Poppy was forcing her to inhale.

Why haven't I seen any cars? Maybe the road is closed up ahead.

Of course, she hadn't seen any cars behind her, either.

"I'll think about it," Teresa said finally.

Not long after that they came to the road that Poppy indicated led to the church. Teresa didn't know what to do. Free continued to sleep and she hesitated to wake him. She didn't know how to behave around

165

him now that they were lovers. He was playing it cool, but she supposed that was only because Poppy was with them. She was anxious to be alone with him again. He had an incredible body and he made her feel as if her body were a diamond to be cherished. Bill had never made her feel that way. He had talked a lot about love and friendship but he'd never wanted intimacy. Probably because he had known from the start that he was going to dump her. He had been biding his time until she was most vulnerable. If she got the chance, it would be fun to flaunt her romance with Free in front of him. It was incredible how swiftly things had happened between them. Then again, she had made a vow never to speak to Bill again.

"You're going to have to slow down," Poppy warned as a road off to their left rushed closer. Teresa found herself hitting the brake, although she didn't want to. Free stirred at the sudden deceleration. Teresa flipped on her blinker and turned off the main road.

"I don't know why we have to see this man," Teresa muttered.

Free opened his eyes and yawned. "Where are we?" he asked.

"We're going to church," Poppy said.

Free was not impressed. "Did she talk you into stopping, Teresa?"

"More or less," Teresa said.

"You don't have to see the priest, you know," Free said. "It's not a requirement. I've never seen him."

Teresa smiled. "I bet you've never been in a church in your life."

"That is an astute observation," Free agreed.

"Poppy's worried that the road farther north is blocked," Teresa said. "What do you think?"

"I think if we drive fast enough we'll be able to break on through to the other side," Free said.

"If it is blocked, you might be late to your show," Teresa said. "We might have to head back south and circle around. That could take a long time."

Free yawned again. "I'm not worried about it."

"What did you say was the name of the club where you're going to be doing your show?" Teresa asked.

Free glanced over. His eyes were bloodshot with fatigue, but his mouth looked fresh. She wished she could kiss him right then. He'd know how to make her feel better.

"We're booked into Club Bardos," he said. "I don't see how you could have forgotten the name."

Teresa laughed. "It's been a long and exciting night."

Free nodded. "And it isn't over yet." He paused. "What are you going to tell the priest?"

The trees around them were beginning to thin. It was a relief in a way to Teresa; they had begun to make her feel claustrophobic the last few miles. In the distance she could hear bells chiming. She rolled down her window. The rain had stopped and the moon had come out, shedding much needed light. She smelled flowers: daisies and roses and carnations.

"I'm not Catholic," Teresa said. "I don't have to tell him anything."

"That's the spirit," Free said.

The church had to be a Spanish mission because it couldn't be anything else in that part of California. Yet it wasn't. It was like no mission ever made. The thing could only have been a cathedral lifted from the center of old England. It was constructed of fat square-shaped granite blocks. There were people milling around outside it, *lots* of people, and the sun hadn't even begun to show its face yet. Teresa was confused beyond belief. Two alien structures in one night. A witch from the twilight zone and now a priest from God knew where. She really should just have gone to bed and not tried to run away from home when it was raining so hard.

"Park over to the right there, away from the people," Poppy said. "They're not used to cars here."

"How do they get here then?" Teresa asked.

"They just show up," Poppy said.

"Losers, all of them," Free remarked.

"Are you coming in with us?" Teresa asked him.

He laughed. "Give me a break."

Teresa parked and climbed out with Poppy, stretching her legs and back. One thing she did have to admit, the smells were delightful. Yet she could see flowers nowhere. She suspected the gardens were in an inner courtyard. The church and adjoining structures appeared to have been built around one. Free reached in the backseat for his garment bag.

"I thought I'd change so you wouldn't recognize me when you get back," he said.

She stuck her head back in the open window. "I'm only doing this to make Poppy happy," she said softly so that Poppy couldn't hear.

"You don't have to make her happy," Free said, also whispering. "You only have to make me happy."

She grinned mischievously. "It's my pleasure to do

that." She started to stand back up. Free reached over and grabbed her arm. He studied her intently, the change in his expression dramatic.

"I'm going to need a favor from you soon," he said.

"What kind of favor?"

"You'll see. Can I count on you?"

"Sure."

"For anything?" he asked.

"Absolutely," Teresa said.

He released her. "Good."

Teresa walked toward the cathedral with Poppy by her side, the main bell tower rising high above their heads. Teresa could not understand how she had not seen pictures of this building—it had to be one of the most impressive structures in all of America. But she didn't ask Poppy to explain the riddle to her because every time Poppy spoke she created another riddle.

"Don't talk to any of the people except for the priest and me," Poppy warned.

"Why not?" she asked.

"It wouldn't be a good idea, trust me."

"I don't trust you. I don't know why I'm doing this. Do you know why?"

"Yes," Poppy said. "You're here because you're tired of driving."

"That makes sense. Hey, can I ask you something and please give me a straight answer. Were John and Candy real people?"

"Yes."

"How did you and Free know them so intimately?"

"We were very close," Poppy said.

"You answered sarcastically when Free asked if he

had narrated the end of their story accurately. Had he?"

"No, but he didn't lie. It's complicated."

"Can you tell me what really happened, from what you know?"

"Maybe later," Poppy said.

Poppy did not steer them to the massive front doors of the church, but rather, to a side entrance that opened into a hall and then into the courtyard Teresa had pictured. They passed two old nuns playing with a child tossing pennies into a fountain. The other people milling about were incredibly nondescript, to such an extent that it made Teresa wonder what was wrong with them. There wasn't one of them that stood out. Certainly, they paid her and Poppy no heed. It was as if they had stumbled upon the church and were content to walk around outside in the moonlight and let time pass. Teresa again wondered what time it was. She regretted once more having lost her watch. The sun would have to come up soon, she thought.

The opening led into a hall that led into a courtyard and Teresa got to see the flowers she had whiffed a mile away. They were gorgeous, but not structured in neat and tidy rows; rather, growing free around a maze of bushes and trees; the flowers she had smelled and others as well: phlox and lilies and birds of paradise, poking their beaks out of green branches that sparkled with drops from the recent rain. She would have liked to have enjoyed them for a bit but Poppy urged her forward. They entered the church from the side.

A Catholic Mass was in progress. People sure got up

early in these parts, she thought. The rows of pews were endless, and at least half full. Most of the people in attendance were older, except for the choir at the back on the upper level. Teresa couldn't see them clearly, but from the sound of their voices many must have been children. Their responsive lines echoed through the vast hall, as the priest up front spoke in thundering Latin.

Latin?

That was supposed to have gone out years ago.

They reached into wooden bowls stationed near the door, filled with holy water, and blessed themselves. Teresa had to follow Poppy's example to get it right.

"Is that your father leading the Mass?" Teresa asked softly, instinctively feeling the blasphemy of talking in such a sacred place. She nodded toward the altar, shimmering with gold and silver under the warm light of a thousand tall white candles. The odor of incense was strong, penetrating. Teresa could feel it inside her brain.

"No," Poppy whispered. "My father generally takes confessions at this time." She nodded down a side aisle, which branched off at various points into smaller private chapels with altars, where candles could be lit and offered for the blessing of a specific saint. Poppy led her forward. Teresa reached out and clasped Poppy's hand, although she wasn't sure why. The dark was not so thick that she couldn't see where she was going. Poppy squeezed her hand in return and flashed her a quick smile. It was the first time Teresa had seen her display anything more than melancholy or boredom. She regretted her comment to Poppy of a moment ago, that she didn't trust her. She realized Poppy had not wanted to stop at the church for her own sake, but for the sake of Teresa.

But confession? What do I have to confess? Even if I did have something, why should I do it now? In this place?

They came to a wooden door, an undistinguished door given the scale and eloquence of the church. Poppy nodded. "He's in here," she said.

"Aren't you coming in with me?" Teresa asked.

"I can't."

"Why not?"

"It's something you have to do on your own," Poppy said. "I could only bring you here."

"Who says?"

"It's the way it is." Then Poppy did something most unexpected. She reached out and hugged Teresa. She actually kissed her cheek. "Tell him everything," she whispered in her ear. "Be an open book and listen to what he has to tell you. Above all else, don't be afraid. He's here to help you."

"But why do I need help?" Teresa asked as Poppy released her.

Poppy smiled again and patted her shoulder. "Ask him. Be brave, be honest." She nodded. "He's waiting for you."

Teresa opened the door and stepped inside.

The room was small and cozy. There was one window, a stained glass scene of Jesus sitting on a hilltop surrounded by a group of children of all races. The window was closed, but Teresa knew it faced the courtyard. The hint of light behind the window surprised her, though, because if the sun was coming up, it wouldn't be rising in the west. The window glowed with warm yellow light, nevertheless, and was most enchanting. A vase of fresh flowers stood on the windowsill, filling the room with fragrance.

The priest was approximately fifty years old. He sat in a simple wooden chair beside the window reading a book by the light of a nearby candle. Dressed entirely in brown he had thin silver hair and a ruddy expression. He looked up as she entered and his gray eyes were kind. He closed his book and motioned for her to sit on the chair in front of him.

"Hi," she said, crossing the room and sitting down. The chairs were not so close together that she felt cramped. She crossed her legs and let the warmth of the room seep into her. Her shakes and nausea began to subside, though her wrist continued to throb. The priest smiled faintly, and she added, "Poppy wanted me to talk to you."

His smile widened. "Do you want to talk to me, Teresa?"

She paused. "How did you know my name? Did Poppy call you and tell you I was coming?"

"In a manner of speaking. But you'll find I know a thing or two about you. I don't say that to make you nervous, it's my job to know."

Teresa felt uneasy. "I already met a woman tonight who knew everything about me. I didn't like her. She scared me."

The priest was gentle. "Do I scare you?"

She considered. There was truly a warm and loving atmosphere in the room. It was as if she had finally come home after a long adventure.

"No," she said. "You seem like a nice man. But I

have to tell you up front that I don't know why I'm talking to you. I'm not a Catholic. I've never been to confession before." She made a helpless gesture with her hands. "I wouldn't know where to begin."

"Maybe I can help you. I understand you were recently involved with a young man, and that the two of you broke up and your feelings were hurt."

Teresa shrugged. "I'm getting over it. It's no big deal."

"But it is a big deal to you."

She smiled. "Can you read my mind?"

"I can see the pain on your face. Tell me about it, Teresa."

Teresa considered. He was perceptive, she had to give him that. She figured there'd be no harm in talking to him about what Bill had done to her. She had talked about little else all night.

"All right," she said. "Bill was my boyfriend. He was the first boyfriend I ever had. I cared about him a great deal, and I thought he cared about me. He acted like he did. He helped me get a singing job at a well-respected club near the beach. He gave me confidence in myself, something I never had before. But it was all ruined when he cheated on me behind my back with my best friend, Rene."

"You say he gave you confidence in yourself. Did he do anything else for you?"

"He did a lot of things. He made me feel things I had never felt before. He bought me things, small gifts. He went out of his way for me. Once I was sick and he took me to the doctor when . . ." Her voice trailed off. "But I did a lot of things for him, too. I was totally devoted to him. He was not devoted to me."

"Why wasn't he devoted to you?" the priest asked.

"Because he was a jerk, that's why. I'm sorry, but I think that's what it boils down to."

"Before he met your friend, Rene, did you feel he loved you?"

"He told me he did. I believed him. But it was just another lie."

"Do you feel he loves you now?"

She made a face. "No way. He wouldn't have dumped me so easily."

"Was it easy for him?"

She forced a laugh. "I think it was a lot easier for him than me."

"Go on, Teresa."

"Well, it hurt me. I felt like I wanted to die. I can't tell you how much it hurt. It was like I was living a perfect fairy tale and I was so happy and everything was so perfect. But then—bang! Wake up, girl. The dream is over. Your boyfriend is sleeping with your best friend."

"How do you know Bill was sleeping with Rene behind your back?"

"I caught them."

The priest was surprised. "You did?"

"Yeah."

"When?"

"Today."

"When did Bill break up with you?" the priest asked.

"Today. Well, it's early Sunday morning right now. He actually dumped me Saturday evening. Rene was there, at my parents' apartment. He gave me the news and then he left with her."

"Did you see him after that?"

"No. I mean, yes." She lowered her head. "I saw him, but I didn't talk to him."

"Because you found him in Rene's arms?"

A tear ran down her face. "Yes."

"Tell me about it. It will help."

She sniffed. "How will it help?"

"You have to feel your pain before you can offer it to the divine."

"How do you offer your pain to the divine?" she asked.

"You just do it. It's easy. It's the only way to deal with situations that are too painful to bear. But first you have to accept what is real. Tell me what really happened, Teresa."

She looked up into his kind gray eyes. She had just met him, she didn't even know his name, but she would have liked to have had him for her father, even if he was a priest. He had the most gentle voice.

"All right," she said. "I'll tell you."

Teresa lay on the floor a long time after Bill left with Rene. It was dark when she finally sat up and looked around. The apartment was empty, and she did not expect her parents back until the following evening. She had nothing to do and no one to do it with. That was not going to change, she thought. Bill was gone. Her Bill, taken from her by her friend—and he was not coming back.

But that thought—*Bill is gone for good*—was not that clear in her head, nor were the other thoughts. She wouldn't let them be. The ideas floated in and out of her awareness in the form of, *Bill's going to be harder to talk to now,* or, *Bill doesn't know what he's doing,* and, *I'm going to kill those two.* She was sad beyond words, she was madder than hell, and she was confused. Her confusion was vast. She thought if she could talk to Bill again, maybe just for a few minutes, things would become clearer. He had said something about not wanting to leave her at that time, so he must still care about her. He couldn't want to end it just like that. He had never even slept with her for godsakes.

Teresa went into the kitchen and got herself a glass of water. The lights in the apartment were off. The dark was of peculiar comfort to her. It shielded her from things that would have been too harsh to look upon at the moment.

Just before she left the kitchen, her fingers grasped an object—a steak knife. Her parents loved steak, but she enjoyed only fish and chicken. She was a semi-vegetarian. She picked up the steak knife anyway and a powerful image—it was so clear, so strong, it might have been a vision—of her stabbing Bill and Rene flashed through her mind. She saw the blade cutting through their flesh, felt their blood spurting over her arms. Yet the image was so grotesque it made her shudder and she pushed it away.

The knife. What did she do with the knife?

She had slipped it into her back pocket.

Why?

There was no why. She was upset.

She left her apartment and drove to Bill's house. For a long time she just sat in her car and stared at the place. All the lights were off. Bill's car was parked out front—beside Rene's. She had no trouble recognizing her best friend's vehicle, but she didn't fully comprehend what it signified. Oh, she knew it probably meant Rene was inside with Bill, but that they were together, *really* together, was hard for her to fathom. Even Bill couldn't have forgotten her that fast.

She eventually got out of the car. At the front door of the house, she didn't knock. She had a key and just went inside. Bill's parents, she remembered, were away for the weekend. It was kids' weekend, she thought. Anything goes.

Anything at all.

She found them in the family room. Lying on the floor in front of a smoldering fire. Lying together asleep beneath a patchwork quilt, their faces blank under the spell of sleep. She stood watching them and they didn't move once. Their breathing, though, she could hear that. The sound of air going in and out of their lungs annoyed her. She was confused, but she knew this much: they weren't supposed to be sleeping together.

She took the knife out of her back pocket.

The steel of the blade glowed red in the faint light radiating from the low flames in the fireplace. The *vision* she'd had in her kitchen returned as her mind began to clear. What was there to be confused about? This afternoon she had been Bill's girlfriend. Tonight Rene was his girlfriend. Three minus one equals two. The mathematics were simple. Goodbye, Teresa, and thanks for introducing us. You were finally good for something. Bill changed partners like he did shirts, she thought in disgust. He'd have a hard time, though, taking off the shirt he was wearing now if there was a knife stuck through it—all the way through to the inside of his ribcage. Rene also would have a difficult time combing her beautiful black hair if it was soaked with blood. Dried blood was known to cause hard-to-manage knots.

Teresa didn't know which one she hated more.

She stepped into the family room.

"Then what did you do?" the priest asked.

Teresa was embarrassed. "I came to my senses. I'm no killer. I dropped the knife and ran out of the house. When I got home, I packed an overnight bag and got in the car and started driving. I picked up Poppy Corn and her friend, Freedom Jack, just before I got on the freeway." She shrugged. "And now I'm here. That's my confession."

"Are you running away from home?" the priest asked.

She had denied the question all night, but it was harder to lie in the presence of this fine man. It seemed he had an intuitive sense for when the truth was bent. Lowering her head, she sniffed again. Her face was still damp from her tears.

"I am, yes," she said.

"Do you know where you're running to?" he asked.

"No."

"You're going nowhere."

He was not asking her. He was stating a fact. She raised her head. "I suppose I'll end up somewhere," she said.

The priest surprised her. He shook his head. "Not

necessarily. You're in trouble, Teresa. There's nowhere left for you to go."

Suddenly she was having trouble breathing. The confessional room that she had found cozy only minutes ago now seemed claustrophobic. Even the smell of the flowers was bothering her, making her sinuses swell. Something had begun to clog her head. Pressure grew in the center of her skull. It grew as her heart throbbed there—the same throbbing she had experienced in her wrist.

"I don't know what you're talking about," she said. "I've done nothing wrong. I dropped the knife and left Bill's house."

"Are you sure you dropped the knife?" the priest asked.

"Yes. Positive. I wouldn't lie about it."

The priest sighed. He looked down at the book, resting closed on his lap. It was an old volume, with a cover dried with time. She couldn't tell if it was a Bible, though. There was no title on the outside.

"The worst lies are the lies we tell ourselves," the priest said. "We live in denial of what we do, even what we think. We do this because we're afraid. We fear we will not find love, and when we find it we fear we'll lose it. We fear that if we do not have love we will be unhappy. But the nature of God is love. The nature of God is happiness. We are a part of God, and because of that we have nothing to fear." He looked at her and smiled gently. "Relax, Teresa, and tell me what happened. I will not judge you, no one will. I am not asking you to confess. I am only asking that you drop your state of denial."

Teresa was perspiring heavily. "But I've told you everything I know. I did not stab them—I wouldn't have done that. You have to believe me."

"What did you do then?"

"I left! I ran away! I got in my car, went home for a few minutes to pack, and ran away from home! What do you want from me?" She burst out crying. "I can't tell you what I don't remember!"

The priest was interested. "Is it that you can't remember something?"

"Yes! I can't remember what I did with the knife!"

The priest leaned forward. "Let me help you remember. This is where you are having trouble. You left Bill's house. You—"

"Stop!" Teresa cried, jumping to her feet. "I have to go. I'm sorry, but I can't go through this. I don't deserve this. I've done nothing wrong except be abused. That's my only crime, father."

The priest took her in with sorrow on his face. "It's a crime to be abused," he said.

"You're damn right it is."

Teresa strode from the room. Poppy was waiting outside, kneeling in a pew beside the confessional booth. She could have been deep in prayer for all Teresa knew, or cared. But Poppy jumped up and chased after her as Teresa hurried from the church, out into the fragrant courtyard, and then back toward the front of the church. Teresa had eyes only for her car. She needed to get in the car and get away as fast as she could. She had felt that way at her apartment.

"What happened?" Poppy gasped, running to catch up with her.

"I learned that the road up ahead is blocked," Teresa said. "But it doesn't matter. We can break on through to the other side."

Poppy stopped dead in her tracks. "That's what they all think."

CHAPTER 13

THEY WERE IN THE CAR DRIVING NORTH AT HIGH SPEED,
the road deserted in both directions. The rain fell
again, in torrents now. Poppy was silent in the backseat. Free fidgeted in the front, wired to the max. He
had changed into a black suit with a red hat. His
garment bag lay folded on his lap. It appeared to be
empty. He was talking about a place up ahead that he
said she had to see.

"They have great food there," he said. "You can get
anything you want. The service is wonderful. They
have an incredible wine selection. There's no waiting,
either. Only a few people know about the place."

"It sounds nice," Teresa muttered, distracted. The
expression of sorrow on the priest's face continued to
haunt her. Of course, he was a nice man, but he'd had
nothing really important to say to her. She didn't
know why Poppy had been so anxious for her to meet
him. He'd been way off talking about her being in a
state of denial. She hadn't done anything wrong—

what was there to deny? Anyway, how could you expect a priest to understand relationships? They were all celibate.

The sky was growing lighter.

Dawn was not far off.

"It's just up ahead," Free continued. "I've been here before. There's nothing you want that they don't got." He slapped the dashboard. "Hell, they even sell money, it's that full-service kind of place."

"Neat," Teresa said. She spoke to Poppy. "Have you been there before?"

"Once," Poppy mumbled. "For cigarettes."

Teresa laughed, although she didn't feel much like laughing. She was so close to throwing up that she had to drive with the window down even with the rain blowing. "We'll be sure to get you cigarettes," Teresa said.

"Don't bother," Poppy said. "I'm trying to quit."

"It's here!" Free shouted, pointing excitedly. "Turn off here. Wow, I can't believe it. We made it. I was afraid we were never going to get away from that goddamn church."

"What turnoff is this?" Teresa asked, squinting through the pouring rain. She must have the name of the road wrong. It couldn't be—

"Bardos Lane," Free said.

"But isn't that the name of the club you're supposed to play?" Teresa asked. Free laughed hysterically.

"Yeah!" he said. "We were closer than we thought. What a break. We're already here. Amazing."

"But you said the club was in San Francisco?" Teresa said.

"I was wrong," Free said, rubbing his hands fiendishly together. "We don't have to go any farther. We can satisfy all our shopping needs here."

"Our shopping needs?" Teresa asked.

"Yes," Free said. "We're going to a mini-mart. I love mini-marts. And this one's my favorite. Oh, there it is! Make a left up ahead, Teresa. Let's just you and I go inside. We don't want Poppy with us. She's in a grumpy mood and she'll just spoil our party."

"You don't want to come in, Poppy?" Teresa asked, as she pulled to a halt in front of the store. Free's excitement bewildered her. The mini-mart was like a million others in the world. It appeared to have no special qualities. Yet she was relieved to see it. She figured she could buy some aspirin and maybe something to settle her stomach. She was through with Junior Mints for the night.

"No," Poppy said.

"You should at least get out and stretch," Teresa said, opening her car door. Free was already outside and standing in the rain, getting soaked. He was the craziest guy.

"I stretched my legs at the church," Poppy said flatly.

"Have it your way," Teresa said, climbing out.

Free hurried her to the door of the store, which was good given the amount of rain coming down. But just before they went inside, under the shelter of an overhang at the front of the place, he stopped and wanted to talk.

"Remember I asked if you could do me a favor and you said yes?" he asked.

"Yeah."

"You told me you would do anything for me?"

"I will. I like you a lot, Free."

He leaned over and gave her a quick kiss. "And I love you, Baby. But I need a pretty big favor at this stop. I'm only asking this cause I know you and I are going to be together for at least a long while and I'll need the money to take care of you and love you and you just got to help me out, you see, cause Poppy won't, she never would, and that's just the way she is and I can't change it. Do you understand?"

Teresa chuckled. "Hold on, you're confusing me. What favor can I do for you? Just tell me and I'll do it."

"Do you have your knife?"

"My knife?"

"Your mother's steak knife? Didn't you say you had it in your back pocket?"

"No, I don't know what you're talking about." She smiled. "The only thing I have in my back pocket is that joker you put there when you pinched my butt."

"Check it out," Free ordered.

"What?"

"Check in your pocket and see if you've got your knife. I might need you to use it in a second."

Teresa stuck her hand in her pocket, just to prove that she didn't have a knife. Because it was a ridiculous assumption. She didn't walk around with a knife, and besides, she couldn't have sat in the car for the last how many hours with something as long and hard as a steak knife snugged up next to her.

Ouch!

A hot pain stabbed at her left hand, the one she had thrust in her pocket. She quickly pulled it out to see that it had blood on it. Free was right. She poked more carefully into her pocket with her right hand and drew out the knife. It *was* the same knife she had taken to Bill's house.

"I can't believe it," she gasped.

"Let's get inside."

"But I'm bleeding!"

"We'll get you a Band-Aid." He grabbed her arm. "Come on, we don't have much time. The sun's starting to come up."

They entered the store. A tall man with chestnut brown skin, a white goatee, and a bald head stood behind the counter. He looked half starved, like an Ethiopian who had seen one drought too many. He nodded in their direction but didn't speak. Teresa thrust her knife back in her pocket, out of sight. Free quickly dragged her around the store collecting beer, doughnuts, a carton of milk, and Junior Mints. She started to tell him that she didn't want any candy, but before she could speak he was already piling the articles up on the check-out counter, and besides, he had just pulled out a gun and was pointing it at the tall African.

"Give me everything you've got," Free said calmly, staring the man in the eye. "Or you won't have to worry about renewing your health insurance policy."

"Free!" Teresa screamed.

"Don't tell him my name," Free said impatiently. "We are robbing this store. If you identify me to him he'll be able to identify me to the cops. I can't let that happen. I'd have to kill him before I let that happen."

"But why are you doing this?" she cried.

"Keep the bills coming," Free said to the man, who was nervously emptying the register on the counter, beside the beer and the doughnuts. Free continued, speaking in her direction, "I am doing this because I need the money. I'm in love with you and I will have to support you for the next sixty years. Also, there's some fine white powder I've grown very fond of and it costs more than you can imagine." He paused and his head whirled in the direction of the door. "Take out your knife. We are about to have company. Do it!"

Teresa withdrew the knife from her pocket. Why, she didn't know. She wasn't going to hurt anyone with it. She had never hurt anyone in her life.

A young woman walked into the store. At first Teresa thought it was Poppy. They were about the same height and had the same long dark hair. But this woman was a few years older. She wore a nurse's uniform. Her eyes grew big when she saw Free with a gun.

"Stay!" Free shouted to her. "Get your hands up. Move over to my partner. Slowly! Don't try anything funny or your boyfriend is going to be sleeping alone tonight. Cover her, Baby."

Teresa stood helpless. "I can't."

Free shoved her in the direction of the young woman. "Don't argue with me! Stick your knife at her throat and keep it there."

Teresa slipped behind the woman and raised the tip of the blade to her neck. The woman shook with fear two inches in front of her and Teresa was grateful that she couldn't look into her eyes. Teresa felt as if reality had fractured into a million insane pieces. Free was such a great guy. She had slept with him for godsakes! But here he was, a common thief, like John. A heroin addict, too, maybe—no wonder the guys had been friends.

This cannot be happening.

Sirens sounded in the distance.

No, they weren't that far away.

"Jesus Christ!" Free swore. "Not again. Teresa, grab her by the hair and don't let her go." He started to scoop the money into the pockets of his black coat, his gun still leveled at the man. He shouted at the store employee. "You! You back up! You get your hands up and don't look at me!"

"Jack," Teresa pleaded. She had taken hold of the woman's hair to pull her closer, even pressing the blade more firmly against her throat, but she was losing it. She was one inch from fainting. The store whirled around her like a merry-go-round. The sirens screamed. Everything was happening so fast. The cops were practically on the doorstep!

"We're going to have to make a run for it," Free yelled, dollar bills falling out of his pockets. He backed away from the tall man. "We can't leave any eyewitnesses—we're going to have to kill them, baby."

"No!" Teresa cried.

"Yes!" Free cackled. He was having a good time. "We'll waste them and drive back to L.A. and spend all our money in all the wrong places." Free shook his gun at the man. "Say goodbye to truth, justice, and the American way."

"No!" Teresa screamed.

Free shot the man in the face. The bullet entered his nose and left behind a shattered mound of red dripping tissue. The man fell far and hit hard. Free threw his arms in the air and whirled in her direction.

"Slit her throat!" he ordered.

"No!" Teresa cried.

"The word is yes!" Free laughed. "Open her veins! Yes! Make her bleed! Yes! Do it! The police are coming!"

"Don't ask me to . . ." Teresa began, but she didn't get to finish because the young woman suddenly tried to struggle free. Perhaps she figured her odds were poor just standing around, and Teresa would have privately agreed with her. But in the woman's struggle, she shook forward and the knife Teresa had at her neck *accidentally* cut her a little bit. It was definitely an accident, but it wasn't exactly a tiny cut. Because the neck was chocked with big important veins and the blade was razor sharp and—well, Teresa cut her bad enough so that the blood began to flow. Bad enough so that the woman collapsed on the floor the moment she shook free of Teresa's hold. Free laughed as he looked down at the nurse squirming at his feet, her hand raised to try to stop the bleeding.

"Teresa," he said. "You did it to her faster and more efficiently than I could have." He raised his gun and pointed it at the woman's head. "But now that you've passed your test there's no reason your second victim should have to suffer."

"You can't," Teresa moaned.

Free shot the nurse in the back of the neck.

The blood and soft tissue splattered Teresa's face.

Free stuck his gun back in his belt. "I can and so can you. Let's quit this place, babe. We can have beer and doughnuts back home. In L.A."

Free grabbed her arm and dragged her out of the store.

Into the failing night, where they saw no police.

They climbed in the car. Free drove.

Teresa stared at the blood on her shirt. A nurse's blood.

Poppy lit a cigarette and stared out the window.

Bored. Poppy was bored and they had just killed two people.

Teresa didn't understand anything.

"This is a fast car," Free said, getting onto the freeway.

Anything that had happened since she had left home.

"We'll be there soon," Free said, heading north.

Even the things she could remember.

"Where?" she whispered.

Nowhere, the priest had said.

"Your place," Free said.

The road led nowhere.

"This isn't the right way," Teresa mumbled.

Because she was in trouble.

"Yes, it is," Free said.

Because she had done something wrong.

"I live the other way," she insisted.

With her knife.

"We'll be getting off the freeway in a second," Free said.

The knife she had not left at Bill's house.

"No," she said. "No."

The knife in her pocket.

"It's the next exit," Free said.

The knife she had used to cut into someone's skin.

"I live three hundred miles from here!" she cried.

But whose skin? Who was really bleeding?

"Get real," Free said.

Bardos Lane. Border Lane.

Teresa's stomach lurched. "I feel sick."

Border World. Bardos.

"We're getting off here," Free said, slowing.

CHAPTER 14

THEY DROVE INTO A RESIDENTIAL AREA. THE RAIN CON-
tinued to fall, but lightly now, as if the growing
daylight was capable of drying up the clouds that had
plagued them all night. They turned into an apartment complex and parked in a carport. Free jumped
out and Poppy and Teresa got out slowly. Actually,
Poppy had to help Teresa up. She was so sick she had
trouble staying on her feet.

"Where are we?" she mumbled.

"Same old Teresa," Free said, striding into the
complex. Poppy helped her as they followed him.

"I'm going to have to lie down soon," Teresa said.

"Yes," Poppy said, her voice gloomy as midnight.

Free led them into an apartment. He had the key.
Teresa collapsed on a couch near the door and closed
her eyes for an instant. To say she was in shock would
have been like saying victims of serious burns were
familiar with pain. Her pain, devastating as it was,
could now hardly cut through the fog she had entered.
They had killed two people. Blood was all over her

clothes. Plus, she was bleeding. She had accidentally cut her left wrist with her knife. Like she had accidentally cut the nurse's throat. Oh, God, Free had just aimed the gun at them and pulled the trigger. All for a few lousy bucks. The sin of it all. Having slept with him, she must now have disease growing inside her.

Teresa opened her eyes and looked around.

The apartment looked familiar. Very.

"Where are we?" she mumbled again.

Neither of them answered her right away. Free was in his glory, skipping around the living room as if he had just found a pot of gold at the end of the rainbow. He had his empty green garment bag in his hand and was unfolding it on the floor. Poppy sat smoking at a table in the adjacent kitchen. Teresa could hear water running. She turned her head with great effort and saw that the door to the bathroom was lying partway open and that someone had left the water running in the bathtub and that it was overflowing.

"Somebody should turn that water off," she said weakly.

"Why don't you do it?" Free asked.

"I'm too sick to get up," Teresa said.

"Always an excuse with you," Free muttered.

She was offended. "You killed those people, you animal."

Free laughed. He was smoothing the wrinkles out of his empty bag. What had he done with his other clothes? Just thrown them away?

"It was fun," he said. "Did you have fun? You killed one of them, too, remember?"

"That was an accident!" Teresa protested.

Free giggled. "What a memory!"

Teresa cried weakly. "Would somebody please turn off that water? The noise of it is hurting my head."

Free paused in his task and approached. "You're the only one who can turn off the water, babe. Poppy and I ain't got no hands." He stopped. "Do you want to watch TV?"

"Huh? No."

"I have a video you might enjoy," Free said, ignoring her. He pulled a tape from his coat pocket and walked over to the VCR. He thrust the tape into the machine and turned on the TV. "You keep asking where we are—and I've already told you. But you can think of this tape as a kind of a road map to the highways in these parts."

"I can't watch anything right now," Teresa whispered, her head falling to one side. She had to struggle to remain conscious and she had to ask herself why she was trying at all. Because if she just blacked out she could forget her pain. It was so tempting, just to escape. Yet something kept her eyes open.

"Believe me, you'll watch this," Free said.

The tape started. It showed a young woman closing her apartment door and striding toward her car in the night. The camera followed the young woman—she was really only a girl—as she threw an overnight bag in the backseat and climbed in. The girl started the car and, looking both ways, pulled out into the rain.

The rain.

Lightning flashed, giving her a glimpse through the damp window.

Recognition. The girl.

"That's me," Teresa gasped, sitting up.

"Yes," Free said. "That's you leaving your house this evening."

"Where did you get that tape?" she asked.

"I have friends in high places," Free said. "I have more friends in low places. Do you want me to rewind the tape?"

"No," she said quickly. "I want you to turn it off. You shouldn't make tapes of people without their knowledge."

Free snickered. "I have a tape of you in the most compromising of positions." He leaned close, and she couldn't imagine how she had thought his mouth tasted fresh. His breath reminded her of a sick patient in a hospital; it stunk of decay. "I have a tape of you naked in the bathtub! What do you think of that, Miss Teresa?"

"You lie!" she swore.

He hooted at the ceiling. "*I* lie!" He spun around, making a dance of it, and skipped back to his bag. "All right, I'll leave you in ignorance. You seem comfortable there." He knelt on the floor by the bag and pulled down the zipper. "An old army issue," he said gleefully.

The bag intrigued her, but not in a good way. She had seen something like it before. "Where did you get that thing?" she asked.

"These bags were used in the sixties and the seventies," Free said. "Many of our finest young men returned home from Vietnam in one of these."

"A body bag," she whispered.

He had been carrying it around all night. Slowly emptying it.

For what?

Wrong question.

For whom?

"Right," Free said with a giggle.

The need to know, even in denial, was what was keeping her eyes open. Teresa got up with great effort and turned on the TV and VCR.

She pressed Rewind. Counted time by the numbers. Then pressed Play.

She was taking a bath. Naked.

"I told you." Free snickered behind her.

A hot bath, with the water running a little so that it wouldn't get cold when she started to get cold. Teresa glanced in the direction of the bathroom where the water was overflowing and soaking the carpet of the hallway. The water was not entirely clear. There was something in it, floating around, but also thinning out. Teresa glanced back at the tape. She was picking up a knife, that young pretty girl. So much pain on her face. But no extra pain as she took the blade in her right hand and cut a deep gash across her left wrist. Pain, so she had believed at the time, was only for the living. There was no need to open both veins. Her parents were out. She had all night to die. The blood spurted silently into the water and the girl leaned back and closed her eyes.

The girl had been wrong about death taking away all her problems.

Teresa turned off the tape.

It all came clear to her in a single moment.

The whole insane night. Of course, there were no witches, no castles, no magical priest. These things did not exist on the planet earth.

"I killed myself," she said.

"Yes!" Free cheered behind her. "And I am here to collect you, my hard-earned reward. That's what I have this bag for."

Teresa stepped toward the kitchen, hugging the wall; she needed it for support. "Is it true?" she asked Poppy. "Am I dead?"

Poppy was pale and exhausted. She ground out her cigarette in an ashtray. "Almost," she said, and the regret in her voice was plain.

Teresa nodded. There was no sense denying it now. She did not need to step into the bathroom to see. There was a girl dying in there.

"How long?" she asked.

"Not long," Poppy said.

Teresa nodded again. No wonder her wrist hurt. She remembered then, quite clearly, opening the vein. Her nausea must mean her heart was running out of blood to pump. "Who are you two?" she asked.

"My name is Candy," Poppy said. "Popcorn and candy, you could call me. That's John behind you." She shrugged. "Sometimes I call him Jack."

"You're both dead?" Teresa asked.

"Yes," Poppy said.

Teresa coughed. "Why are you here?"

"For fun and profit," Free said.

"He was here to tempt you," Poppy said. "At least that's what he thinks. I was here to help you, if you wanted my help." Poppy shook her head. "You didn't want it, Teresa."

Teresa nodded. "How could you have helped me— after what I did?"

"Bardos is the realm between the living and the

dead," Poppy said. "On rare occasions it's possible to make choices here that affect where you go—whether you go anywhere."

"I made the wrong choices," Teresa whispered.

"You cut the poor nurse's throat," Free joined in.

"Shut up," Poppy told him. She turned back to Teresa. "It wasn't so much what you did, it never is. It's what inside. You wouldn't let the truth in."

"You lied about everything," Free interrupted, now airing out the body bag, flapping it in the middle of the living room as if he were getting ready to set up a tent. "You never slept with Bill. He didn't want you. He wanted Rene and you couldn't face it. It's as simple as that."

Poppy slowly stood. She faced Free, who paused in his play with the bag to see what she'd do next. There was suddenly fire in Poppy's usually cool expression. She held out her arm and pointed at him.

"You have a nerve calling Teresa a liar," she said. "After the lies you told tonight. You're a hypocrite."

Free appeared genuinely perplexed. "What lies did I tell?"

Poppy was impatient. "About John."

Free dropped his bag, suddenly angry. "I told it the way it was. I accept what I did, the good and the bad. I don't try to dress it up like Mother Teresa here. Or like you, Poppy. Candy was nothing but a lazy chick with the loyalty of a politician. You prattled on about how she searched for John all those years. If she looked so hard, how come she didn't find him?"

"Where was she supposed to look?" Poppy demanded. "She had no leads—John made sure he left none for her. It was John who ran from her, not the other way around. And why? Because he was embarrassed for screwing up."

"He didn't screw up! He was just trying to help her pass her stupid test."

"John didn't have to hit the teacher," Poppy said. "Even when he did, even when he went to juvenile hall, it wasn't the end of the world. John could have called Candy at Berkeley when he got out. They could have worked something out together. They were strong together."

"John was the only strong one!"

"John was weak when it really mattered!" Poppy yelled. "When he hurt his hand, what did he do? He felt sorry for himself. So he was in pain. Lots of people are in pain. They don't become junkies. They don't blame the world."

Free was indignant. "You don't know what pain is. You cakewalked through life."

"I suffered," Poppy said. "Everybody suffers at one time or another. But I worked to make myself a life. I made mistakes, sure, plenty of them, but I didn't hurt anybody."

"I didn't try to hurt anybody, either!" Free cried.

Poppy clapped her hands together. It was as if she had been steering him in a direction and he had just taken a critical turn. "Yes! That's true. That's the truth *you* don't know. Listen to me, I came here tonight for you as much as for Teresa. You don't belong in this awful place, John. You belong with me."

Free snickered. "I can't go with you after what I've done."

"What did you do?" Poppy asked.

Free chuckled. "In case you've forgotten, I killed you."

"No," Teresa interrupted.

Free glared at her. "You stay out of this."

"No," Poppy said quickly, eyeing Teresa closely. "Let her talk. Think of her as an objective observer. Teresa?"

Teresa pulled herself off the wall with what strength she had left. "I enjoyed the story of Candy's life," she said. "She sounded like a nice person. But it was John's story that kept me captivated. I think it was because he had so much potential and kept missing out on opportunities. Until the end I thought he would turn it around. He would get his act together and find Candy and live happily ever after. I know you told me at the start that they weren't going to be together, but I still kept thinking they would be. Do you know what I mean?"

"No," Free said. "You know nothing. You never even met John."

"But I did," Teresa said. "I met him through you. I got to know him pretty good. He had a hard time. I went through nothing compared to him. I admired him in a way, I really did. But you see, when you got to the part in the store, I knew you were lying. I spoke to Poppy about it, you can ask her. I know that John didn't kill Candy."

"I did!" he protested. "I shot her in the heart." He looked at Poppy. "You tell her."

Poppy shook her head. "She's just told you, John."

He was confused. "But I was there. I know what happened."

"No," Poppy said. *"I* was there. I was in that store with the only man I had ever truly loved. You were there with your self-pity and your guilt. You carried your guilt to the grave. You didn't shoot me. The cop shot me trying to hit you. He killed me, accidentally it's true, but he killed me nevertheless. When I got hit, you did everything you could to hold me up, and keep me from falling onto that dirty floor. Not because you were still using me as a shield. But because you wanted to hold me. You wanted that more than a chance to shoot back, which you could have done. You wanted it more than a chance to surrender and to live. You just wanted to hold me. You died wanting that." Poppy took a step toward him. "Why do you have to play the devil every night for the rest of eternity? You're not such a bad guy. I still love you. Do you still love me?"

Free stared at her as if seeing her for the first time, or perhaps as if he were seeing her after a very long time. Teresa didn't know when they had been alive.

"What did you want to tell me just before you died?" he asked.

"That I named my son after you," Poppy said.

"You weren't making that up when we were in the car?" Free asked.

"I told the whole truth and nothing but the truth."

Free was silent again. Then he took a deep shuddering breath. "Yes," he said.

"Yes?" Poppy asked.

"I still love you," Free said.

Tough cool emotionless Poppy wept. She nodded her head and bit her lip. "Yes," she said, and it could have been the most wonderful sound in the world—in the whole universe—to her. She threw open her arms. "Hold me now, John. Hold me forever."

They embraced. They kissed.

It was wonderful. Beautiful.

Teresa even shed a tear, she was so happy for them. Happy. Such a feeling for a dying soul to have.

None of this changed the fact that she had slit open her wrist.

No ruby slippers. No going home to a dead body.

Teresa felt happy for them but miserable for herself.

"You're not dead yet," Poppy said, looking over at her from Free's arms, reading her mind.

"But you said?" Teresa began.

Poppy separated herself from Free. She positively glowed, as a guardian angel should. Teresa had not realized angels could be so human.

"What did I say?" Poppy asked. "What did the priest say? Did you let him finish? Of course not, you ran out the door. You ran from your mistakes. But had you stayed, you would have heard that all mistakes are forgiven if you offer them to the divine. It's a very deep secret, this one."

"But I don't know how to offer anything," Teresa said.

"There is no how," Poppy said. "The truth itself is a true offering. That would be accepted. What is the truth here? You tried to kill yourself? You can see that now—that you did it out of self-pity. You learned about self-pity from John's story. You demonstrated that right now. Forget about the people you killed tonight. They were already dead. Forget what happened at the witch's house. I don't care. You and Free behaved like children, but all that matters is that you've learned from each other." She poked Free in the side as she spoke. "And to think, he came here tonight hoping to drag you down to the lower regions."

Free smiled. "They're not so bad once you learn the ropes there."

Poppy gave him a look. "Do you want to go back there?"

He scratched his head. "Ah, no." He hugged her close. "I think I'm ready for a change for the better." He paused. "Are you sure I didn't kill you?"

Poppy laughed. "Had you tried to shoot me you would have missed. You were always missing me." She turned back to Teresa. "What am I going to do with you, silly girl?"

Teresa fought a wave of dizziness. "You're not physical. You can't drag me from the tub. I'll be dead by the time my parents get home." She lowered her head. "It doesn't matter what kind of offering I make to God."

"Why don't you make it and see what happens?" Poppy asked.

"But?" she began.

"Go ahead, try it," Free said. "What can it hurt? If it works for you, I might try it myself."

"What do I do?" Teresa asked.

"Feel what you feel," Poppy said. "Then let it go to the divine. It doesn't matter how you think of God. It only matters that you let him think of you."

"Can I close my eyes?" she asked.

"Yes," Poppy said.

"Just don't die on us," Free said.

Teresa closed her eyes. She saw many things in the

space inside. How good her life had been. The gifts she had been given, what with her voice, and her writing, and yes, even her parents. She saw how devastated they would be to return home to find her dead. They had sacrificed a great deal to have and raise a daughter.

Bill was there inside her heart as well, where she had left him when she had fallen in love with him. It was possible that she had to let him go, maybe even never see him again, but that was OK. He had enriched her life. He had not come to destroy her life. He was in love and love was always good. He, too, would be devastated to learn she had committed suicide.

And Rene? That mischievous little devil. Well, girls would be girls, just as boys would be boys. Teresa found she couldn't hate her. She couldn't hate anyone, not even herself. Life was wonderful, it was terrible. It was both things together and that was what made it so special. She was only sorry she had tried to throw her life away.

Teresa felt a great weight lift.

It caught her by surprise. It was just gone—the dread.

Such a blessed relief.

Poppy and Free caught her as she fell.

They carried her to the couch where they lay her on her back.

Teresa opened her eyes. "I'm going to die," she whispered.

"Are you afraid?" Poppy asked.

"No," she said honestly. "I'm just sad that I was so stupid. I was having a good time, really. Another few days, weeks, I would have felt better. I let my emotions carry me away." She coughed weakly. "I just wish I could let them carry me back."

Poppy stroked the side of her face. "Do you want to go back?"

"Yes," Teresa said. "More than anything, I want to live again."

Poppy turned to Free. "What do you say? Don't you think, between one novice angel and one experienced devil, we could bring a spark back into Teresa Chafey's life?"

Free was serious for a moment, staring down at Teresa. "I think it's possible, anything's possible."

Poppy smiled a radiant smile. She leaned over and kissed Teresa on the forehead. "Close your eyes and you will see that spark."

"I will live?" Teresa asked.

"Yes," Poppy said.

"But how?"

"Shh. You will see," Poppy said.

"But why are you helping me? I mean, why you in particular?"

"Why did God send me?" Poppy asked, amused. "Let's just say you're important to someone very important to me. Right now, you have no idea how much you'll be seeing of him."

"But?" Teresa began.

"Sleep." Poppy reached down and gently shut Teresa's eyes. "Dream of living. The dream goes on and on."

There was space, there was time—they existed as they had always existed. Yet it seemed as if she could

go anywhere in either of them—for she had changed.
She didn't seem to have a body, yet she felt someone
nearby. This person, this being, was thinking of Bill,
and so she thought of him as well. Then suddenly she
was in Bill's family room as he slept in front of the fire
with Rene beside him. Teresa could see that they were
both fully dressed. She was happy to see them and felt
none of the crushing pain she had felt earlier in the
night, yet at the same time she felt strangely distant,
disconnected from the scene. Something was about to
happen, and it was important, but she wasn't at all
worried about how it would turn out. Most of all she
experienced great peace. The being she had noticed by
her side a moment ago was still there, even though she
could see no one besides Bill and Rene.

Her attention was drawn to the fireplace. The logs
had long ago given up their fuel to the flames and all
that was left were a few glowing embers. But a strange
alchemy was taking place in those ashes. As she
watched, a miniature cyclone spun in the midst of the
burnt remains and the embers glowed brighter at the
sudden gush of air. Their orange light changed to a
bright red, and the ash chased up the chimney as if
called by an old man in a sleigh. Then came a loud
crack as one of the few remaining pieces of wood
exploded. A spark flew out of the fireplace, through a
split in the grill, and landed on Bill's arm.

He bolted upright from his deep slumber and
looked around him anxiously. He peered directly at
the point from which Teresa was observing him and
rubbed his eyes. If he saw her, he didn't indicate he
had—she certainly couldn't see herself. He brushed
painfully at the spot where the spark had landed on

his arm. Then he suddenly stopped and looked in the direction of the front door. A breeze stirred his hair, it came in from the outside. He stood and walked toward the door. Teresa followed him effortlessly.

The door was lying wide open. There was a key stuck in the lock. It was Teresa's key—Bill had given her one for no good reason. He had painted it gold as a joke, telling her it was the key to heaven. She must have left it in the lock when she had come over to see him earlier in the night.

Bill pulled the key from the lock. He glanced out the door at the street, back in the direction of sleeping Rene. Comprehension crossed his face—and horror. He ran into his bedroom and grabbed his shoes and his car keys. He didn't shut the door as he ran out of the house. Teresa wasn't sure where he was going, but she had a good idea. She wasn't totally indifferent to the proceedings. She hoped he made it in time.

She hoped they both did.

At the family party.

"Oracle James Hospital."

The young man said, "Oh, well..."

EPILOGUE

SUNLIGHT POURED IN THROUGH AN OPEN WINDOW. SHE saw it even before she opened her eyes. Someone was calling her name. She rolled over in bed and looked at who it might be. The handsome face of a young man with dark hair came into her focus. It was funny how her vision was blurred like that, she thought. The guy was sitting in a chair beside her.

What's he doing in my bedroom?

That was just the thing—it wasn't her bedroom. She instantly recognized the anesthetic decor. A hospital—she was a patient in a hospital. She must have driven into a tree or something.

"Hi," the guy said.

"Are you a doctor?" she asked. He was dressed in white, but seemed kind of young.

"No, your doctor wanted me to sit with you. He thought you'd be coming around soon. How are you feeling?"

"I have a bummer of a headache. And my wrist . . ."

Teresa saw the bandage on her left wrist.

It all came back to her in a flash.

All the earthly parts.

"God," she whispered.

The young man stood up quickly. "I'll get your doctor."

"No, that's all right," Teresa said, surprised at the calm in her voice. It wasn't every day you tried to commit suicide; it was certainly a first for her. Yet she didn't feel overwhelmed by the immensity of what she had tried. She just felt slightly embarrassed and silly. She swallowed painfully. Her throat was dry. "Could you please get me a drink of water?" she asked.

"Sure." The guy was happy to do something for her. She seemed to make him uneasy. Another nut case, he probably thought. She would have to reassure him that she was not your normal attempted suicide. He handed her the glass and she drank gratefully.

"Who brought me in?" she asked.

"I think it was your boyfriend. Bill?"

She nodded. For some reason, the news did not surprise her. "He used to be my boyfriend. He's going with my best friend now."

The guy lowered his head. "I'm sorry."

"Oh, it's a drag, I know. It really pissed me off when I found out. I wanted to cut them up into little pieces. But they're probably better off together. Do you know what I mean?"

She was confusing the guy. She must sound way too philosophical considering what she had just done to herself. "Yeah," he said. "Bill and a girl are waiting outside to see you. Your parents are here also. Should I tell them you're awake?"

"In a minute. If you're not a doctor, what are you?"

"I'm a college student. But I plan to be a doctor." He gestured to their surroundings. "This is work-study for me."

She smiled. He was pretty cute. "I hope I wasn't too much work for you."

"You were no work at all. You slept the whole time I was here."

"I tried to kill myself," she said suddenly.

His dark eyes were sympathetic. "I know. You must have been through a lot lately."

She shrugged. "It's been rough. But it gets that way sometimes." She added, "I'm never going to try it again. I just wanted you to know that."

The guy smiled with relief. "That's what I wanted to hear." He stood. "I'll go get your parents."

"Fine." He was at the door before she spoke next. "Wait."

He stopped. "Yes?"

"Why do you want to be a doctor?" she asked.

"Why do you ask?"

"Come on, tell me," Teresa said.

"Well, I want to help people, and doctors make lots of money. I like wearing white." He shrugged. "My mother wanted me to be a doctor."

"You don't look like a mommy's boy to me."

"I'm not." He added, "She died when I was very young."

Teresa felt a pinch. "I'm sorry."

"Yeah, she was a great mom." He opened the door. "I'll be back in a few minutes, Teresa."

"Wait," she called.

He stopped. "Yes?"

"You know my name. I don't know yours. That's not fair."

"You're right. My name is—"

"Wait!" she interrupted.

He laughed at her. "What is it this time?"

"You're Johnny!"

He frowned. "How did you know? I'm not wearing a name tag."

Teresa was also puzzled. "I don't know. I must have met you somewhere before. You look familiar." She glanced at the open window to her left, glad that the sun was out and the storm was finally over. She smiled suddenly. "You look like someone I know," she said.

Look for Christopher Pike's

THE ETERNAL ENEMY

Coming in May 1993

About the Author

CHRISTOPHER PIKE was born in Brooklyn, New York, but grew up in Los Angeles, where he lives to this day. Prior to becoming a writer, he worked in a factory, painted houses, and programmed computers. His hobbies include astronomy, meditating, running, playing with his nieces and nephews, and making sure his books are prominently displayed in local bookstores. He is the author of *Last Act, Spellbound, Gimme a Kiss, Remember Me, Scavenger Hunt, Final Friends* 1, 2, and 3, *Fall into Darkness, See You Later, Witch, Die Softly, Bury Me Deep, Whisper of Death, Chain Letter 2: The Ancient Evil, Master of Murder, Monster,* and *Road to Nowhere,* all available from Archway Paperbacks. *Slumber Party, Weekend, Chain Letter, The Tachyon Web,* and *Sati*—an adult novel about a very unusual lady—are also by Mr. Pike.